by the wayside

stories

by the wayside

stories

by
anne leigh parrish

Attention schools and businesses: for discounted copies
on large orders, please contact the publisher directly.

For information contact:
Unsolicited Press
Portland, Oregon
www.unsolicitedpress.com
orders@unsolicitedpress.com
619-354-8005

ISBN: 978-0998087238
Cover Design: Kathryn Gerhardt

acknowledgments

an angel within — February 22, 2015, *New Pop Lit*

how she was found—Issue 2, October 31, 2016, *The Useless Degree*

artichokes — Winter 2013 issue of *Spartan*

the professor — February 14, 2013 debut issue of *Souvenir*

smoke — March 4, 2015 issue of *Writer's Bone*

where love lies — Issue 3 of *Literary Orphans*

the keeper of the truth — October 2011 issue of *r.kv.r.y*

an act of concealment — Volume 18, Number 1, Winter/Spring 2013 issue of *Crab Orchard Review*

trial by luck — Winter 2013 issue of *YeahWrite! Review*

along came a spider — May 2014 issue of *The Corner Club Press*

by the wayside — Volume 1, issue 4, *Nomos Review*

letters of love and hate — Fall 2015 issue of *Crossborder*

the fall — October–December 2010 issue of *Prime Number Magazine*

bree's miracle — Issue 3.2 of *S/tick*

patience — Fall 2015 issue of *Corvus Review*

fire and ice — *October 7, 2015* issue of *Writer's Bone*
a thing of beauty — May 6, 2016, *New Pop Lit*

To John, Bob, and Lauren

contents

an angel within

Deep in the heart of a dirty, windy city stood a tired, wooden house; and inside the house lived a woman with busy hands; and inside the woman lived an Angel. The Angel sat on the head of a pin. Her balance was poor, and she tended to teeter this way and that.

The woman, Leet, felt this teetering only as a slight twinge beneath her rib. Leet mistook it for the pang of a hungry heart seeking passion as she swept, washed, and sewed. She longed for love to compensate her for the rotten hand dealt her by Fate. Her parents were gone, leaving her in charge of her younger sisters, and though she loved them both dearly, found them demanding and selfish.

The Angel had come to her as a prayer on the lips of her dying mother. *Protect my children*, she had begged as she lay battered and broken in the street beside her husband, assaulted by thugs, relieved of their money and simple jewelry, then kicked repeatedly for not having more valuables on them. These were indeed ugly times.

The Angel saw at once that the protector must be Leet. Leet was twenty, and the eldest. She had a hard edge that made her tough, and enough self-doubt to hold her tongue. Leet's sister, Lisa, was sixteen and obsessed with beauty products, particularly nail polish. She planned to own a nail salon one day, and grieved that her parents hadn't taken her dream seriously. The youngest girl, Layla, was thirteen and liked to wear pretty clothes and carry small, costly handbags that let her pretend she was someone who didn't live in a dirty, windy city where the sun was rare and only grudging at best.

They paid off the house with their parent's meager insurance policy. A miserable monthly stipend from Social Security meant their daughters wouldn't starve. Leet's hopes for a higher education, which had been iffy when her parents were alive, now went the way of the wind. She washed the front windows and watched scraps of paper lift and twirl, then disappear down the street. She hated her life and resented her sisters.

They are your blessing, the Angel said. Leet had by then, a few months later, reluctantly accepted the presence of the Angel within. She knew it was wrong to respond silently with sarcastic thoughts like, *Yeah, with a blessing like that, who needs misfortune?* She recalled her stoic mother, always putting a brave face on things. Leet's father repaired watches. He made enough money, but they were never comfortable. Leet's mother had always fretted. Now Leet was the one who lay awake, adding sums, making disappointing compromises.

Leet bagged groceries in a harshly lit, giant store that required a long commute on two different busses. Leet would have preferred a job closer to home. There'd been none. Most of the customers said nothing to her as she put their items in the sturdy brown paper bags. Some tried to make conversation. They talked about the weather, particularly the snow, which could be unrelenting. Some were crabby, some just downright nasty. Sharp rebukes sat unspoken on Leet's tongue, held there by the Angel who murmured soothing words in her ear. *Let it go; let it go. They know not what they do.*

Oh, yeah? Well, they can kiss my . . . Leet restrained herself. She smiled and wished everyone a nice day.

Her trouble continued when she got home. Her sisters worried her. Lisa was happiest when she had her nail polish bottles lined up on the kitchen table like glamorous beauty contestants, she once said. The choosing took time and patience. Concentration, too. The applying was done with a surgeon's care, if not skill. She often slopped outside the boundary of her nails, just as she'd done with her coloring books years before. Waiting for her nails to dry meant she couldn't do her homework. This happened even on nights when her polish was several days old. Leet finished many math worksheets for her, and wrote a couple of book reviews, too. She was especially good at book reviews, always knowing what the author was saying one layer below the actual words on the page. Lisa had trouble with the words themselves. She didn't understand why people bothered to read books, let alone write them.

Layla caused her share of grief, too. She was arrested for shoplifting. She was detained at the entrance to a department store with three small handbags shoved inside her own large purse. She assumed that because the handbags didn't have anti-theft devices pinned to them, she was in the clear. An undercover store detective had been following her since she left the perfume counter. Layla didn't look like the kind of girl who could afford a store like that, which made her presence there at all highly suspicious. Leet bristled at the explanation. How did anyone know how much money anyone else had? She wasn't defending Layla as much as she was crying out against their own lesser fortunes. Again, the Angel intervened.

Patience, child. Patience!

Leet promised the juvenile court judge that she would better supervise Layla. The bailiff escorted her out. He was punishingly handsome. She smiled her best smile. He was unimpressed.

God is testing you, the Angel assured Leet. *Your fortitude will be rewarded.* Leet knew better than to ask when.

Lisa got herself a nineteen-year-old boyfriend, only a year younger than Leet. He was edgy, sensitive, clearly suffering for some unnamed art. He sat at the table, stooped, silent except when he ate, which he did almost constantly. His dirty dish never made it to the sink unless Leet carried it. She didn't mind, for once. She made small talk, tried to catch his eye. When she did, she was met with a gorgeous sullen stare. Lisa didn't deserve him. Lisa was round in the middle. Leet was not. Lisa had the brain of a lizard. Leet did not. These astounding differences, which she imparted with great delicacy—*You're just a little roly-poly, aren't you?* and *Please save the crossword puzzle for me; I know it's not at all your thing*—didn't impress the boyfriend. Leet overheard him tell Lisa that he thought her big sister was weird.

Leet despaired. She would remain unloved forever. She was jealous of Lisa. She'd known this, but hadn't seen. The Angel chided her. *You must guide your sister in this matter. Protect her innocence.*

What innocence? She's been giving it up since she was fourteen!

The Angel grieved.

So, Leet guided Lisa, cautioned her against

5

losing her heart and doing something she'd regret. Lisa nodded, miles away. Leet also guided Layla. "Get a little job," she said. "Save some money. Then take yourself shopping as a treat. That way, you can reap what you sow." Layla also nodded. Her eyes were full of longing. Contemplating her next caper, no doubt.

Leet ignored the Angel's gentle reminder that cynicism would avail her nothing.

Oh, so what? she thought.

A man at work asked her out. He was older, in his late thirties, with a desperate air about him that made Leet cringe. Loneliness could do that to a person, she thought. The Angel nodded in agreement. They went to a small Italian restaurant where the hearty food made Leet relax. She drank wine, obtained with a fake ID. She giggled. When he asked her all about herself, she told him she was an Angel. She laughed long and hard, causing him to look confused. She didn't explain. It would sound too strange. He wanted to see her again. She said she didn't see why not. He wasn't bad looking. Why his wife had left him she supposed she'd find out in time.

It came to her in a flash of light. She wasn't an Angel, and didn't want to be. She didn't want to be any better than she really was. She wasn't mean-spirited or possessed of a cruel heart, but she'd held her tongue long enough.

She summoned her sisters. There would be changes made. From then on, they were to toe the line. Lisa would improve her grades, or else.

"Or else what?" Lisa asked, her eyes narrow with challenge.

"I'll kick your ass," Leet said.

Lisa sucked in her breath.

"And you," Leet told Layla. "You get rid of those sticky fingers of yours, or you'll get the same."

Layla's heart skipped a beat.

They sulked. Both remembered how in childhood an expression of sadness made Leet show a little kindness. Leet showed them no kindness now.

Then they tried wheedling. They offered to do her chores. One shed tears. The other refused to eat for two whole hours. They gave up and went on with their day.

The transgressions fell in number, then stopped. No more arrests. No more failing grades. Lisa and Layla didn't exactly thrive, but held their own just fine.

And as for Leet, she went on seeing the man from work. The future, which had once been black and without end, took shape. The Angel praised her.

You have found your voice and your true self, she said.

Yeah, and no thanks to you.

On the contrary, this is exactly what we planned.

We? Who the hell is We?

But the Angel was gone, on her way to assist another in distress, leaving Leet, a clever, capable young woman, to find her own answer in time.

how she was found

Fiona was a mouse. Everyone said so. As a child she'd been bookish, lonely, with little to contribute conversation-wise. Her brother, Finn, was outgoing, popular, now the owner of a Mercedes dealership in Pasadena. Why Pasadena? They'd grown up in the Pacific Northwest, both graduates of the University of Washington. He majored in business; she in anthropology. He went home with a college roommate one long weekend, a guy from SoCal as Finn took to calling it, and they had drinks with an aunt in Pasadena. Finn was smitten, not only with the climate, but with the aunt's neighbor, Heather, who was, even Fiona had to admit, the quintessential California girl. All that straight blonde hair made Fiona ache, though her mother (a loyal person for the most part) told her that was just nonsense because Fiona's wild red hair was just as remarkable, if not more so.

That red hair became a beacon on her first dig. In the high desert of Western Mexico, against the glare and green of hot sand and scrub, she was easy to spot from above. The whine and growl of the twin-engine Cessna that bore her thesis advisor, Professor Martin Harris, made the team below look up, shade their eyes, and follow its progress to the landing strip half a mile away. The Professor's presence, even at that distance, caused anxiety to mount. He could be demanding, unforgiving, and harsh. Yet more than once he'd been found weeping over some patch of ground that had yielded nothing of value. Perhaps its barrenness was the cause of his dismay. Or that he drank on the quiet from a silver flask. No doubt sometimes the booze got the better of him.

Nine days before, Fiona had found human remains near the village where the three other graduate students—all male—liked to buy tequila. By then they'd been in country for three weeks and had made that trip half a dozen times. That day, Fiona had gone with them. She said she'd wait in the Jeep. They said she should join them, to get some local color and maybe a local hunk—they were intent on setting her up, it seemed. She demurred. They warned it could be a while because the purchase couldn't be concluded without several rounds of hearty sampling. Fiona was fine. She'd take herself for a walk.

Off the men went one way and Fiona the other. The sky raged blue. She didn't care for sun. At home, in Tempe, she escaped to malls, indoor pools, or the furthest stack of the library, and then when she couldn't avoid going out, she hated how cruelly the heat pushed her down.

She followed a faint trail into the foothills, smelling creosote and sage. The saguaros were everywhere, like sentries. At the base of a boulder was a chunk of white stone loose enough to pull free. She examined it. She loved rocks. She'd wanted to become a geologist, but her father objected. Anthropology was better for her, he said, offering no defense of his opinion.

Some earth fell where the stone had been removed, and Fiona probed the opening, hoping for more quartz or maybe amethyst. She had read that amethyst had been found nearby. She hungered for a trove.

What she unearthed was a bone, part of a human hand. Fiona had studied hand bones in depth at the Arizona State University, where she was pursuing her Master's Degree. Her obsession with hands had earned her some unflattering nicknames from the men on the dig, one of which, "hand-job Fiona," rankled.

She put the bone back and took in the three-sixty view so she could remember the landmarks for later. She intended to get Professor Harris out there as soon as possible, assuming he'd take her remarks to heart. His custom was to overlook most of what she said. Fiona had slowly come to realize that she'd been included only because the awarded grant Professor

Harris obtained specified the need for gender equality in selecting his staff.

The three men wandered up the road in a state of cheerful disarray. From her vantage point, Fiona heard their voices but not their actual words. In the lead, as always, was Kurt, Harris' favorite and the likely co-author of his next book. Behind Kurt was Jack, who insisted on being called Jackson, *to make up for being so short*, Fiona thought. Last in line was Tom. Fiona was in love with Tom. He was rugged, strong, spoke gently, and gazed at her with eyes she might describe as limpid. Along with geology, Fiona had also considered majoring in English, a notion that drew even more resistance from her father than the suggestion of studying rocks. If Tom suspected Fiona's affection for him he gave nothing away. Fiona planned to conquer his heart by the time they went back to Arizona. The trouble, aside from the fact that he might not find her in the least attractive, was Tom's fiancée, Maricelle, about whom he spoke incessantly—so much so that Kurt and Jackson, and even Harris one night around the campfire as his flask made another appearance, called him "pussy-whipped."

Fiona joined the men on the road, told them what she'd found, received vague words of approval, then drove them back to their dig site where they'd uncovered pottery fragments, tools, and decorative pieces of petrified wood. They had hoped to reveal a settlement of native peoples dating back a thousand years. The year before, a large one had been found a few miles away, in the opposite direction from the village, by a colleague of Professor Harris, Arnold Sand. Sand's paper had led to a new understanding of how that part of Western Mexico had been populated. Professor Harris decided that he should locate the next one before Professor Sand did, and was delighted when the grant came through from the National Science Foundation. He was considerably less delighted with the meager find.

When Fiona shared her news with Professor Harris, he grew quiet, withdrawn, obviously deep in thought. He asked to be taken there. He and she went alone. The light was failing but Professor Harris insisted they press on. When he saw the bone, he used the walkie-talkie on his hip to contact the three men they'd left behind. They were to pack up and prepare to change locations first thing in the morning.

For the next nine days, they camped outside the village and uncovered the rest of the skeleton. She consisted of a damaged skull, one clavicle, one scapula, four ribs, a broken femur, shattered humerus, an intact pelvis—the shape and proportions of which identified the body as female—and a total of sixteen additional hand bones. There were no clothing remnants with her, strongly suggesting that she'd been in the earth long enough for all to disintegrate. Two objects were close by: a piece of petrified wood, similar to those found at the initial site, and a fragment of a clay pot on which part of a larger decorative pattern had been inscribed.

Now, their time in Mexico was at an end. Professor Harris had just returned by plane from Morelia, where he'd arranged to ship the bones north in two more days. The team would leave then, too. He strode up the trail. He pointed at Fiona.

"I could see you from half a mile up. Why the hell aren't you wearing a hat?" he asked. He and the other men all had on the same kind: wide-brimmed and secured under the chin with an elastic strap. Fiona had brought one, and worn it for only three hours on her first day. She couldn't adjust to how hot it made her head feel.

She'd burned badly. Her skin had finally stopped peeling. That Professor Harris should take an interest in her welfare at this point was odd. Then she realized they might have to appear on the local television station back home to recount the details of their marvelous find. She'd look terrible with her red skin and white rings around her eyes from her oversized sunglasses. That assumed, of course, that she'd even be included.

Kurt, Jackson, and Tom clustered around him. They always did that, forming a male circle with Fiona on the outside. She had stopped trying to penetrate. She prepared a statement to explain her lack of hat, then realized the professor no longer expected one.

He rubbed his hands together.

"This has been an amazing excursion. Tonight, we celebrate," he said.

"Celebrations require supplies," Kurt said.

"Check the back seat."

Kurt and Jackson went and returned with a box. It held three bottles of tequila and six Dos Equis.

"I know tequila's not your drink," Professor Harris said to Fiona.

Fiona didn't like beer, either. She figured she could struggle through one, for the sake of fellowship.

They dined on roasted goat. Fiona had developed a taste for it. Professor Harris had brought back bell peppers, potatoes, and corn, which Fiona carefully chopped, cooked in a large pan, and seasoned with salted butter and hot sauce.

Later, as they sat draped gently by night, Professor Harris invited each team member to share his thoughts. No one offered anything.

"You must have some observations to make. Kurt, you first," Professor Harris said.

"Hotter than hell down here."

All agreed.

"Excellent tequila," Jackson said.

The men agreed.

"Gorgeous night," Tom said.

No one agreed, though Fiona wanted to.

"Your turn," Professor Harris said to her.

"I'm just wondering who she was," she said.

"Until we get her in the lab, all we know is that she's just a woman, presumably at least a thousand years old, who died from some sort of blunt force trauma," Professor Harris said.

"Why was she apart from the others? I mean, why were there no other bodies found near hers?" Fiona asked.

"Maybe she'd gone on an errand and was attacked by an animal," Kurt said.

"Or a person," Jackson said.

"A man," Fiona said.

"It's definitely possible," Tom said.

"What if the carbon dating proves she's not ancient at all?" Fiona said.

"Then we're fucked," Kurt said.

"Nonsense. We found her, we dug her up. We practiced the techniques we've learned," Jackson said.

"Grant money isn't for practice runs," Professor Harris said. He took a long, leisurely pull from his flask. "Besides, if she's not what we think she is, then she's something else, at least," he said.

The men laughed. Professor Harris did, too, once he realized how stupid that had sounded.

"What you mean, I think, is that even if she's younger than we thought, it's still noteworthy. Say she's only five hundred years old. What do we know about the people who lived here then? We'll need to find out. It's a win-win either way," Jackson said.

Professor Harris nodded his approval.

"My mom will be glad. She thinks it's all very murky, living off grants. She says I should have gone into business with my dad," Tom said.

"What's he do?" Professor Harris asked.

"Sells paint."

"Mine taught third grade. Hard profession back then for a man, surrounded by women all day long," Professor Harris said.

The night deepened, and the sky was thrown with stars. Fiona wondered what the others thought when they looked up and saw them. She'd never been one to make wishes. The woman they'd found—

Estrella, Fiona called her—would have looked above to her namesake and wanted to tear one down from that black vault and hold it, just for a moment. She wouldn't need to keep it forever, knowing that anything from nature belongs forever to nature and to nothing else. She wasn't a possessive person, Fiona decided. Larceny or covetousness did not cause her death. She'd been the object of someone's unrequited love. When the affection wasn't returned—because her heart was for another—she'd had no choice but to leave and make her way alone in the desert wilderness. Her would-be lover tracked her down. Even as his weapon was held aloft, he said if she relented and became his, he would spare her life. She wouldn't. Her refusal was the end of her.

She was aware that someone was speaking to her.

"Your family," Kurt said to her.

"What?"

"He asked about your family."

"Who did?"

"Tom."

"Oh. Well, my dad's retired. He was a civil engineer. Dams. 'Damn dams,' he used to say. My mother's an artist, sort of. They still live in Seattle. They wish I'd move back. That my brother would, too."

"Where's he?"

"Pasadena, selling cars."

"To the little old lady from Pasadena."

"Huh?"

"The Beach Boys song."

"Ah."

Silence fell. Fiona tasted her beer. It wasn't horrible, though it had warmed up in her hand. She forced it down. She knew she'd need it later, somehow. Something was going to happen tonight. Something big. Maybe she would declare herself to Tom, for whom her feelings were stronger than ever. And there was hope. He'd complained that very day that he didn't think Maricelle would be all that glad to see him. The others had teased him, saying it would be because he'd look like shit after living outdoors for almost a month. But there was genuine concern in his eyes. They must have quarreled before he went away. She hadn't wanted him to go, and he'd gone anyway, saying it was his future that was at stake. Maricelle might be used to more money than Tom was likely to earn as a professor or researcher. She'd had a better offer in his absence. That was easy to see. Tom had shown them all her snapshot. She was a stunning brunette, as olive skinned as the native women they saw walking along the roads.

"What's your brother's name?" Tom asked.

Fiona's heart leapt.

"Finn."

"As in Huckleberry?"

"Yeah."

"Finn and Fiona. That's quite a mouthful," Professor Harris said. The others laughed.

Fiona finished her beer and went to the cooler for another. The ice had melted. The carton of eggs Professor Harris had obtained was soggy. Fiona took the beer and returned to the group. She felt funny, all loose in the head. It was the beer, she knew. She avoided alcohol as a rule. She was enjoying its comfort now, as people throughout time had. Estrella must have had her version of it. What did she drink to forget? Or to remember? For suddenly Fiona was flooded with memories. She and Finn, trying to outdo each other playing badminton, or throwing horseshoes, or shooting darts in their father's private study. Finn always won. She went in tears to her mother, who told her not to compete with boys. She should learn how to sew or paint pottery. Her mother's plates and vases were all over the house, not very well made, but lovingly turned on the wheel and carefully glazed. Once, in a state of unnamed misery, she'd thrown a few to the floor, then refused to clean up the pieces until Fiona's father ordered her to.

Fiona was aware that the men had stopped

talking. Their unshaven faces were still, bathed in dim firelight. Fiona stood up. She wavered. She went to her tent, which she shared with Kurt. She sat on her cot. Despite the beer, she was too keyed up to sleep, so she went into the tent where the bones had been laid out. She set her battery-powered lantern on the ground, then sat down next to it. Even though she was missing so much of herself, Estrella looked stately. Fiona was mad to know what kind of clothes she'd worn, if they were plain or rich with color. And what about jewelry? Even simple women loved jewelry, though she was sure that Estrella hadn't been simple at all, but calm and totally self-possessed. Fiona put on a pair of latex gloves from the box in the corner and picked up the skull. It had a hole on one side, probably her fatal blow. She stared into the ridged, empty eye sockets and conjured a pair of warm brown eyes with long, inky lashes. Estrella would have been beautiful, far more winning than Fiona was, though Fiona wasn't ugly and she knew it perfectly well. She just had no dash. Nothing that drew attention.

"You need to get a life," Estrella's skull said. Fiona shook so much that keeping a grip on the skull required great effort.

"Stop living through other people, and just do your own thing," Estrella said.

21

"I don't know what my own thing is."

"You'll figure it out soon."

"Why are you telling me this?"

"Who else am I going to tell? Those lunkheads out there?"

Fiona sat with the skull in her lap. It stayed quiet for a long time. Then it said, "Go to bed. Strong women need their rest."

In the morning, Kurt gave a quick yelp when he realized Fiona was on her cot with her arm curled around the skull. He summoned the others. Professor Harris said not to wake her and ruin the moment.

"Wish I had a picture," Tom whispered. Professor Harris motioned for him to go get his camera. Fiona opened her eyes before he'd even left the tent in search of it.

"What the hell are you all staring at?" she asked.

"You and your little friend," Jackson said.

Fiona picked up the skull and stroked it lovingly.

"She was lonely, lying over there all alone," she said.

Fiona got up. Her hands were sticky from wearing the gloves all night. She returned the skull to its proper place in the adjacent tent. The men followed her and waited outside while she put it down.

"That was pretty fucking badass," Kurt said.

"Didn't know you had it in you," Tom said.

Fiona snapped off her gloves. She was hungry. She asked who was going to make eggs. Professor Harris volunteered.

Everyone in the Anthropology Department had heard about Fiona's night with the skull by the time they returned. No one disapproved. In fact, her reputation soared. She had nerve, she had guts, and what about that totally unexpected off-beat sense of humor? She was just the kind of person you needed out there in the field.

As for Estrella, she turned out to be older than anyone expected, over two thousand years. She shed new light on the history of the native people in that region. Professor Harris quickly applied for and received another grant. Fiona was the first team member he approached. But she wasn't interested. She was giving up anthropology in favor of her first love, geology. When her father once again objected, she told him she wasn't asking for permission or even money, since she was okay with going into debt for something that important. He was so surprised, he said nothing, and for once Fiona had the last word.

artichokes

My mother loved artichokes. She trimmed the stems and steamed them in a shallow pan. When cool, she paired them with a vinaigrette sauce. One by one we gently peeled off the leaves and dipped the tender part in our individual glass bowls. Eventually we made our way down to the heart. This was her favorite part, but it was too bitter for me, so I always let her have mine.

My father was gone. He'd left years before to marry someone else. At the time, my mother just sat at the table, another round of artichokes before her, and said she always knew he would abandon her.

After it became just the two of us, my mother found new ways to serve artichokes. She removed all the leaves and went straight to the heart, which she chopped, diced, and puréed with spices and cream to make a spread for bread. Though tasty, it bore little resemblance to the plant it came from. She might have been serving anything, the way she disguised the pungent flavor.

Such was her deceit. "I drove him buggy," she said when I demanded to know why my father had left. This implied a lot of nagging and demands, which I couldn't specifically recall.

The artichoke is related to the thistle. As a child, I had a fear of thistles. The sight of them, out on a walk, made me cringe and scurry away. Their pointed leaves were to blame. I touched one once, loving the purple flower. My hand was bloodied.

One summer, there were no fresh artichokes. Some blight or pestilence had made them impossible to come by. My mother bought canned, which contained hearts only, no leaves, little flavor. "Not at all like the real thing," she declared, giving some to me, then to herself. She always had the good grace to serve herself last. Since I still didn't care for hearts, I gave her mine. She seemed grateful, though didn't say so.

My mother had a secret. She confessed it in her last hour. I was the only one who heard. She'd been in love with a number of different men while married to my father. He knew, and bore it. But not the last one. Maybe my mother's attachment was too strong; maybe he finally saw the hopelessness of a future with her.

While I never knew for sure, I remembered my mother talking fondly of a neighbor, a man in a white T-shirt mowing his lawn and waving at us, and my father staring at the table when she brought him up. My mother and this man were on some neighborhood committee aimed at improving traffic circles and crosswalks. At home she was distracted, lost in thought and inaccessible, which is how people are when they're in love.

The fresh artichokes returned, but too late. I had moved out by then, on to college and disappointing jobs, and my mother lost interest in them. She brought them home from the store and left them in a wire basket to rot. I found them on my increasingly rare visits, and threw them away.

My mother's confession about the neighbor was startling. Then it brought everything into focus. The silent dinners, the long time spent in the kitchen, sorrow finding expression in peeling, cutting, and dipping into what was meant to ameliorate and enhance. And perhaps did. I could never tell.

After my mother died, I was served an artichoke at the home of a friend. The flavor was pleasing as I went down and down, leaf by leaf, until there was no place left to go. When, after the smallest hesitation, I bit into the heart, it was not as bitter as I remembered.

the professor

Something about him is familiar. You see him as you wait for the train. This wait is a daily affair, so you know which chair to sit in, which size coffee to buy. Yet you're not calm, despite the easy routine. This ghost has come into view, for one, and you're also expecting a phone call—the most important one you'll ever get.

The adoption agency is supposed to tell you if the baby you met four months before in Russia will be yours. Dealing with Russians has been a learning experience. Communication is sporadic. Conduct is governed by a system of flattery and payments, not always of money. The counterpart of your adoption agency there suggested that a case of single malt scotch would help your petition. A Hermès scarf for the woman overseeing the infants was a nice touch. Formula for all her little ones waiting for love, twenty-two boxes worth, let you learn that the parents are of "good stock." You're not interested in the parents or their lineage. You just want what they gave up, and your eagerness is clear by the way you hold little Katya (whom you'll rename Katie the moment she's on American soil). Usually, though, money is what moves the process forward. You've spent thousands of dollars already. And now you're spending this money all alone because the man you were going to raise this child with bailed out. It's your fault, really. You have a bad habit of choosing partners who are all flash and no substance, slippery souls who hate being pinned down. You'll do better next time, you're sure. You stood at the window of your apartment and watched his back as he crossed the street with his bags. Well, only one bag. But it was heavy, and he leaned against it hard, sort of how he always leaned against the weight of your commitment to the future, and to him.

Is that what makes you watch this other man now? The way he walks? He, too, leans, but he's not carrying anything. He's a lot older, and his hair is bushy, wild even. All that, adjusted for what he would have looked like twenty-five years ago, makes you look harder. No one else could possibly have quite that combination of dash and decay.

It's Professor DeLille. No doubt about it.

When you are fourteen years old, you live on a cul-de-sac in a quiet college town. The lawn is level in back and slopes in front, where your mother dotes on two huge peony bushes that give gorgeous, fleshy pink flowers. From the curb to the house is a brick walk your father had laid the year you were born. Your initials are set in a thick wedge of mortar on the bottom of three short steps at the very end, where visitors park their cars.

Your mother informs you to expect a house guest. You're put out. You're an introvert and don't spend much time in anyone else's company. Sometimes this trait worries both of your parents, but you've fallen off their radar recently, and the nagging about getting together with friends stops.

The guest is Jean-Jacques DeLille. He's a visiting lecturer in French at the university where your father teaches organic chemistry. Your house is large, with not one but two extra bedrooms for the children your parents hoped they'd have after you and couldn't. Your parents offer their home to people like Professor DeLille, new in town, with no place of their own just yet. Such generosity makes them look good, like team players. They've felt like outsiders for a long time, your parents. You don't understand why. They have friends. People come to dinner. They play golf with another couple whose son is your age. You've been forced to spend time with him before, under the bored gaze of a babysitter who leaves you alone so she can talk to her boyfriend on the phone. The son smells funny and picks his nose. How grateful you are that you don't need babysitters anymore, that your time is your own.

Until now.

You have to prepare for this professor. The bed

needs to be made, fresh towels put in the downstairs bathroom. Your mother consults cookbooks to see what might be tempting and bring pleasure. Your father stays out of the way. He wants very little to do with the professor.

Yet that first night, your father is charming. Professor DeLille compliments the martini your father mixes, then gratefully accepts your mother's offer of wine. She goes to the liquor store and badgers the poor sales clerk into recommending a fine, but reasonably priced, Bordeaux. The professor is tall and broad, not your idea of a Frenchman. You assumed he'd be short and squat, and ridiculous in the bargain. The professor isn't ridiculous. He's commanding, easy to look at, even to listen to with his charmingly thick accent.

You go through his things when he leaves for campus the next morning. There are letters you can't translate, a travel clock, an elaborate shaving kit, boxer shorts, two suits, several silk ties, a pair of polished wingtips, cologne that makes your throat itch after you bring it to your nose, linen handkerchiefs, a light-weight blue bathrobe, a small photo album with pictures of a woman and a boy you assume are the family he left behind (you wonder why he hasn't brought them, given that his appointment is for a full year), and a fountain pen—blue lacquer with gold trim. You imagine him sitting in a café somewhere, writing words of love with that pen, pouring out his heart and soul to another woman, not the one in the picture, someone who's aloof and self-centered, with very short hair, a perfect frame for her hard yet flawless face.

Life takes on a rhythm. Your father and Professor DeLille go to campus in the morning. Professor DeLille presumably looks for an apartment in the afternoons. You say "presumably" because he seems very comfortable in your home, with your mother there to wait on him. You find the change in her marked. She's no longer cold and snappish, but warm and full of life. When the men return, the evening begins pleasantly and only improves as the hours pass.

Thinking of those days, as you watch the older, frailer Professor DeLille cross the tiled walkway of the train station, you become uneasy. You check your cell phone and see that, of course, there's no activity because you would have felt it buzzing. Maybe the deal fell through. Your money lost. Your man gone. You're alone, dejected, miserable.

Get a grip! Just bad memories taking hold. The old sense of abandonment.

Professor DeLille takes a seat and opens a newspaper. His slacks ride up to reveal hairy shins. His shoes are worn. Has he fallen on hard times? Or just become lazy about his appearance?

The time he spent getting ready in the morning, and then again before the cocktail hour! You aren't inconvenienced, because you use a different bathroom upstairs. His is downstairs. But you are always aware of the door closing and the interval of time that passes before it opens again. Your mother always seems to be listening, too. She has to time breakfast and dinner around the sound of that door. She doesn't time your meals to anything. Rather, you meet the schedule she sets. Now she watches and waits for Professor DeLille. She never serves breakfast in her bathrobe. At dinner, she wears makeup.

One day, several weeks into his stay, he takes an interest in you. Fixes you with a bright, curious eye across the table and asks what you want to do with your life.

Your mother watches you closely. She's already told you not to sound like an idiot when an adult asks a question or makes the foolish mistake of trying to engage you in conversation. They're only being polite, she assures you, so there's no point in trying to sound clever.

"I wish to help the poor children of the world," you say. Your father closes his eyes for a

32

moment. Your mother stops chewing the veal she's prepared with lemon and white wine. Professor DeLille continues to assess you.

"A most worthy goal," he says, then resumes eating.

He doesn't ask you anything else. You're sorry you've broken whatever connection might have been possible. You think after a bit that Professor DeLille might be an important person to have on your side, though you don't know exactly what that means.

It doesn't matter, because your mother claims him. He understands how needy she is, and is good at pouring it on. He never fails to compliment the dinner, her dress, her hair, her choice of furniture; though in all honesty, the furniture is old and banged up. Some people, your father included, think it bad taste to have things that are too nice. Their presence suggests that you aren't a serious person. Your father is very afraid of not being taken seriously, yet is highly respected. It's as though your father has found something he was very afraid of losing, though the means of that loss are unclear.

Then the event takes place, the one you regret for years. Professor DeLille has a bad day. You don't know why. That information is never shared. He comes home in a dark mood, speaks little, eats less. He drinks a lot, though, more than is customary. Not one but two martinis before dinner. Not two but three glasses of wine with your mother's duck à l'orange. Then a nightcap of cognac, which he drinks alone on the sun porch—your mother's fancy name for a screened-in outdoor space that the approaching winter makes uncomfortable. You watch him there, by himself, slouching in a wicker chair. Your parents are in the kitchen, speculating. Maybe his appointment has been cut short? Or there's been bad news from home? Your mother aggressively scrapes the plates into the trash— no one feels much like eating, except you, of course— and suggests that a woman is involved. Your father thinks not. He'd have heard about a woman, if there was one. In that small little world of the university, such a thing can't be kept quiet for long.

You go out to the porch. Maybe you can draw him out, get to the heart of the matter. You'll be a hero in your own house! Your sensitivity and compassion will be remarked on time and again. Yet when you stand there, next to his chair, awash in the alcoholic, sweaty smell of him, you can't speak. You want to withdraw at once, and find that you can't.

He gazes at the twilight sky, a view that doesn't inspire you much because of the neighbor's ramshackle house and the overgrown bushes around its front walkway. You realize that your eye is drawn to the world's flaws, not its glory, so you begin examining this trait, wondering how it affects you and your chances for future happiness in life. Professor DeLille turns and looks up at you. His eyes are moist, red-rimmed. A sick man's eyes, you think, someone broken apart from the inside out. He puts his glass on the unpainted wood floor and takes your hand. The shock of it nearly takes your breath away. His palm is callused and rough, damp with sweat. It's an ugly sensation, and the pit of your stomach lurches.

"Come to me," he says.

"What?"

"Tonight. When they're asleep."

He drops your hand. You get out of there. You say nothing to your parents. The evening winds down. You stay in your room, and even lock your door. You lie awake most of the night, listening. There's nothing, only the wind, the furnace running then shutting off, a metal trash can dropping to the ground, probably the work of a raccoon.

Professor DeLille is himself the next day. He looks at you from time to time with complete innocence. You're sure he'd forgotten the whole thing.

The fall progresses, and life takes a sharp turn. When Professor DeLille finally moves out, into an apartment overlooking the lake, your mother goes with him. She confesses to being in love. Your father sits for hours, silent and stunned.

He's unapproachable. He's barely able to make his way to campus every day and teach. You tell him he has to, that he must go on.

Your mother tries to explain, when you see her. She asks you to join her on the long, low couch with its view of the water, cut then with whitecaps below scudding winter clouds. The fabric of the couch is coarse, nubby, something modern and in-vogue, yet hideous. Like your mother's love affair with the professor.

Your mother talks of unhappiness, years of dread and desolation. She's talking about her marriage. Your memories of her at home aren't consistent with this dramatic, bleak landscape she describes. Either she's lying, or she's put on a brilliant front all those years. You don't know, and don't care. All that matters is that you are left in the wake.

Your father carries on the best he can, which isn't very well. He's passed over for promotion and takes a job at a different college, not as good, out of state. By then you're of age and on your own. You haven't been back to your home town since.

While your father slides down, Professor DeLille moves up. He takes a position at Harvard. In the years that follow, you visit your mother and the professor only once at their home in Cambridge. Then Professor DeLille falls in love with someone else and disentangles himself, which is easy, since he and your mother never married. In her letters to you, she speaks of her bad judgment, her failure to recognize the "type" of man Professor DeLille really was. She also writes about your father, and her grief over his unhappiness. She never blames herself for it, though. She never goes that far.

You check your cell phone once more just before it buzzes. The call is the one you've been waiting for. Katya is cleared to leave Russia and will be in your arms the day after tomorrow. You make your heartfelt thanks, reconfirm the essential details, conclude the call, put the phone away, and stand. Your train is only a few minutes off, and you'll use that time to make yourself known to Professor DeLille. You approach with a steady, confident stride, then stop. It's the expression in his eye as he regards a young woman sitting across from him that brings you up short. You've seen it before. It's a hungry look, predatory—desperate, really.

Come to me!

And what if you had? Would he have been satisfied and not turned his sights on your mother? Or would he have had to conquer her, too, before getting his fill? You've pondered this question many times and never found an answer. Now, with him only a few feet away, you're certain you will. He'll give it to you. You won't let him deny a thing. You won't let him slip the noose. In a few more seconds, his eyes will find yours, and he'll know he's caught.

Then you turn away before he sees you, because it doesn't matter. The past is over and done. It's the future you need to focus on now, and the kind of parent you'll be, the lessons you'll teach Katie about what to go after and what to avoid, with everything you've learned of life close at hand.

smoke

Ten years ago there were four, maybe five fires a season, but that month alone there'd been ten. Global warming was to blame. Insects had moved north and killed off the Douglas fir. When lightning struck, those dead trees burned right away. A healthy, living tree was harder to ignite.

Most fires were small and insignificant, in remote, unpopulated areas. Now the three dotting the mountains over the Methow Valley had merged. Five thousand acres scorched, then seven, then ten. The sky dulled, the haze thickened, all views obscured, even from the Lodge, up at 1,800 feet.

Guests were disappointed. Every morning there was an updated smoke map posted on the front desk. After studying it intensely, many checked out. The business group that had booked months in advance complained, asked for a discount, or better yet, free drinks, then went on with their seminar. They were there to talk about trends in resort properties: where the market was hot and where it had cooled off. Right on schedule, three times a day, they showed up in the dining room, wanting to be fed. They looked out the insulated floor-to-ceiling windows at the valley. Those who'd been there before remembered the green, sculpted hills, and the trees lining the river bank around the bend and out of sight. Now there was only the smoke.

Jordan had served in that dining room for the past three years. She was lucky. Valley kids didn't have many chances for a paycheck. Summer was high season. When the forest wasn't aflame, families came to raft down the river or put their little ones on gentle, old horses to be led around the paddock. When the kids got shunted off into any of several Lodge-sponsored activities that were well-supervised—never mind that episode before Jordan's time when the camp counselor lit a joint and shared it with whomever of his young charges was brave enough to try—Mom and Dad could drink champagne at the spa, or whatever mindless pastime appealed to them. Winter was quieter. The few families that came were excited at first. They pretended to know how to cross-country ski, and to enjoy the freezing sleigh rides—with bells on the horses, no less—but then the thrill of snow and icicles quickly wore off and voices turned high and whiny. Then there were the hard-core athletes, skinny men and women of all ages, who carbo-loaded at breakfast, skied twelve miles, collapsed in their soaking tubs, and took over the bar until it closed at 2 a.m., by which time Jordan was long gone, down the winding road to her grandfather's ranch and the back room she'd occupied since the age of ten, when her parents went down in a tiny plane on their way to Montana.

As a young person in the valley, she was one of a dying breed.

Many left for Seattle. Then the recession hit, and it made more sense to stay home. Now the city was in the middle of another building boom, thanks to Amazon, and restaurants and bars really picked up. Jordan often thought of joining the Seattle scene. Her grandfather, Peter, said over his dead body. He had no use for liberal thinking and big government ways that were rife west of the Cascades. Once, Jordan sought to enlighten him. She pointed out that it was, in fact, the rural counties in the rest of Washington State that received more federal tax dollars per capita than in the Puget Sound region. He wouldn't hear any of it. This country was built on self-reliance, not government control. Jordan remembered a time when her grandfather could discuss just about anything calmly—except certain boys she might be interested in or a local initiative to limit access to handguns. But over the last year or so, his mind had stiffened as badly as his arthritic hands, and his words were always short and cross.

"You really should take him to a doctor," Trevor, her on-again-off-again boyfriend, said.

"He's been. Nothing to say, really. He's just

getting old," Jordan said.

That wasn't entirely true. Dr. Nate, as he was called, suggested to Jordan in private that her grandfather's memory problems—forgetting where he put his keys or the day of the week—might be completely normal for a seventy-four-year-old man, but bore watching. He didn't use the word Alzheimer's. Jordan had considered it for a while.

They were on Trevor's porch. His parents' home sat high on a hill. Their view wasn't as good as the Lodge's, especially now with all the smoke, but stirring enough. Trevor's father sold real estate, big parcels to rich people from the city who wanted weekend getaways. He single-handedly turned the valley into a vacation retreat, which made some people happy and enraged others. Jordan's grandfather was one of the cranks.

Those pinheads, coming out here in their fancy SUV's. People like that, who don't get their hands dirty, wrecking the whole damn place.

Anyone who owned a restaurant or pub loved having them, though. Money was money, and it didn't matter where it came from.

Trevor sipped his beer. He was tall and broad, a basketball player who'd tried football and dislocated his shoulder the first semester at college. That had set a bad tone; he lost interest in his classes, dropped out after two years, and came home to do essentially nothing. Finally, his father thought to teach him the basics of real estate, starting with property appraisals. There were some appraisers who could be counted on to come up with the right value and some who couldn't. It was necessary to know who was who. Same with mortgage bankers. Since the crash, they'd gotten awfully fussy about checking a person's credit right down to the bone. One late utility bill could throw the whole deal. Trevor was soon desperately bored. He took to riding his dirt bike over his property, which worried his mother and his father said he needed a good kick in the pants. Then Trevor had the smart idea to apply for transfer to another school, out of state. He'd been at Washington State University in Pullman. Party central, he called it. Majoring in business was easy, but he felt if he continued he'd end up working for his father, which he couldn't stand. He was bright and had good test scores. He put an application in at Stanford. In his essay, he said his time off had been spent learning his father's business, which he loved, but had soon realized that true success in life must be founded on completing his education. He got accepted.

Jordan knew going to California would probably be the end of their relationship. That was okay. When she struck out on her own, it would be better to travel light. Her dream was to go to Seattle and act, or recite free verse in coffee shops, or anything else that would let her pretend she was someone else, from anyplace else where people's boots weren't always dusty, the sky held the promise of rain not drought, and the noise of traffic filled the deadly quiet she had come to hate.

"I hear they might have to close Highway 2," Trevor said.

"Really?"

"If the fire jumps the road, they won't have a choice."

Highway 2 was one of the few roads through the mountains. People liked it better than I-90 because it was more scenic, except now, of course.

In the distance, the sound of a forest service helicopter cut through the gray air.

"You'll be stuck here like everybody else," Jordan said.

"Nah. School's weeks away. It'll all be under control by then."

It had already been a month, and the burn area was growing every day.

"If you say so," Jordan said.

"You just don't want me to go."

"Sure I do."

"You'll miss me."

"Of course."

"Liar."

Trevor lit a cigarette.

"As if the air's not bad enough," Jordan said.

"Tell Grandpa that."

"Deaf ears."

Pete looked upon smoking as an inalienable right, along with life, liberty, and the pursuit of happiness. He'd smoked for fifty years, and said he never felt better. He coughed constantly, especially first thing in the morning—long, syncopated hacks that made Jordan cringe. Sometimes he couldn't catch his breath and wheezed so roughly Jordan was sure he'd hit the floor. His fingers were yellow, the walls of their ranch home stained and streaked. The smell was in Jordan's clothes, her hair, and deep in her nose. No air freshener lifted the stench. And now, with the fire drawing near, the smell of his cigarettes, rather than being blended or masked, only became sharper and viler.

Trevor finished his cigarette and dropped the butt into the top of his beer can, where it made a quick, satisfying hiss.

"Gotta go. Meeting the guys in town," he said.

"Okay."

He stood up. Jordan did, too. She went on her way.

As she drove down one side of the valley and up the other to the Lodge, she thought about the wrangler who'd asked her out. Dwayne was the real deal, the kind of guy her grandfather loved. He'd been around stock animals all his life, grew up right there in Central Washington with a stint in Iraq—another thing that would win him points with Grandpa—and seemed gentle and kind. The horses loved him, at any rate; as did the petrified riders he took out on the trail. And he sang at the cowboy camp dinners the Lodge put on twice a week. He had a deep yet twangy voice made for country music.

Jordan hated country music. All that cheap sentiment over and over again.

Grandpa listened only to right-wing talk radio, which she couldn't stand, either. She already had enough hate in her heart without being encouraged to carry even more.

A week later she accepted Dwayne's invitation.

His idea of a first date wasn't exactly as she'd hoped. She imagined a white table cloth at *Yvonne's*, the Valley's finest. Yvonne herself frequented the Lodge. She was from California, the Bay area, though with ties to L.A., too. Short and slim, she had the energy of a rushing bird in the bush.

Dwayne cooked for Jordan himself instead. His place was small: a one-bedroom cabin in the woods with the sound of the river through the open windows, and of course the smell of smoke. His kitchen table was covered with a red and white oilcloth. It belonged to the Lodge, one of many used on their popular cowboy camp dinners where guests could travel either on horseback or in a horse-drawn wagon along the creek to a quiet, green clearing and eat steaks, beans, corn, some sugary dessert, and listen to Dwayne strum his guitar and sing songs of the Old West. The plates were borrowed, too, the same blue speckled tin used by those rich, bored guests. Jordan had worked many of those dinners, herself. She studied people from the shelter of the cooking shed. The adults looked at their watches while Dwayne sang. The children fidgeted, then broke free from the picnic table and ran around.

Jordan politely ate her fried chicken, paid many compliments, and thought herself an idiot for expecting anything fancy. Then she felt bad for denigrating Dwayne in her mind. She wasn't used to anyone doting on her, she decided. No one ever had. Except her dog, Larry, a fat yellow Labrador who looked at her with vacant, loving eyes. She felt bad when she remembered him. He died the year before.

As for Grandpa, well, he was a case. Not exactly

the doting kind. Dwayne wanted to know all about him. As Jordan predicted, they were kindred spirits.

Yes, said Jordan, he'd served his country—Korea, to be exact. And he'd been married over thirty years, until his wife died. Dwayne was fascinated by the idea that Jordan had been raised by her grandfather. Did she remember her parents at all? he wanted to know, with a suddenly sappy expression which suggested he'd had too much beer.

Not really, she said, although she did. Especially her mother—Pete's daughter. *Watch out for that old fuck,* she'd say with a laugh, a beer in hand, a sway in her hips when Jordan's dad wasn't in the room and they were alone. Which they usually were, in the cabin at the end of the property. Grandpa, in his grief over his daughter's death, tore the cabin down.

He kissed her cheek gently, as if she were about three years old.

Jordan spent the night. She knew beforehand that she would. Dwayne must have known it, too, because he made it a point to mention that he'd put clean sheets on the bed. The sex left her cold, though Dwayne seemed to enjoy himself enormously. Maybe it was gratitude, Jordan thought, that made him clutch her so desperately. He fell asleep right away, and she lay awake a long time. Just before she finally relaxed enough to drift off, it occurred to her that he might be in love.

The white flower in a glass at breakfast proved her right. He said he'd loved her from day one. Jordan didn't understand. She wasn't the kind of woman men fell in love with. When she said so, he looked baffled. He had a dish towel slung over one shoulder. For a moment, it looked like he might go down on one knee.

"Do you doubt me?" he asked.

She shook her head. He placed the flower behind her ear. He danced her across the tiny room and held her a little too hard.

He drove her home and came in with her. He introduced himself as Jordan's boyfriend.

Grandpa was delighted. He'd never liked Trevor.

"Maybe now I can marry her off," he said with a chuckle, exhaling a plume of smoke, followed by a wrenching hack.

Dwayne turned red.

"Don't worry. He always jumps the gun," Jordan said.

Grandpa waved her away. The wooden arms of his plaid easy chair had smoothed to a high shine. The whole room was like that, old and worn. Every time someone came to visit, Jordan saw it in that unflattering, miserable light. The carpet stained black in places. The curtains were missing hooks, making them droop across the sagging rod. In the kitchen, where Jordan opened a couple of beers, the linoleum raised in several places and cracked in others. As a child, Jordan seldom thought of the house and how it looked. Then, it was just a house. Over time she grew to hate it, particularly the way it smelled, not just of smoke, but something stale and damp, even though the climate was for the most part fairly dry. She knew the house would be hers one day. Grandpa said so often enough. Whenever she complained about how it looked, he'd say, "When my time comes, you can fix it up any way you like. Then you'll quit your griping." Jordan liked to think she had an eye for decorating and design. When the Lodge was renovated just the year before, she asked the consultants a lot of questions. The ones who took time to answer taught her a lot. If she had her way, she'd knock down the wall between the kitchen and the dining room to make one open concept space. A bright paint color on the walls would do wonders. And no more drapes; slatted shutters were the thing. All of this assumed that she could live there with the memories. The memories she denied and which took pleasure in burning through her defenses.

Grandpa talked to Dwayne about the fires. They

were still raging; every day seemed worse than the day before. The Lodge would have to close if the wind shifted enough. No sooner had one blaze been put out than another—always from a lightning strike—took off. Men came from all over the west to fight. Their trucks lined the winding mountain roads and the faces of the men going up were clear and tense. The faces of the men coming down were sweaty and smudged. Jordan thought they were thrilling, those men. Fighting fire took a lot of courage, certainly a lot more than raising cattle or singing cowboy songs.

Jordan went out into the yard to be alone with her thoughts. Grandpa and Dwayne were getting along just fine. *Like a house afire*, Jordan thought, then felt stupid. She was not an original thinker. She'd been told this before.

"You're as dumb as a fencepost," Grandpa was fond of saying. What passed for affection from some folks was a true mystery. She could count on the fingers of one hand the people who had been truly nice to her.

One, her mother. But not her father. He wasn't mean, just absent. He worked on a fishing boat out of Seattle. Her parents argued about it. Apparently, her mother didn't like the long time away. "You could ranch with my dad," she'd said, then immediately took it back. Jordan's mother always wanted to leave and move to the other side of the Cascades, and never got the chance.

Two, Lorna, the housekeeper at the Lodge. She was a cheerful waddler, with arm flab that swayed. Sometimes Jordan went with her to make sure the maids had done their job right. When they didn't, Lorna said, "Well, I'll be a son of a sea cook!" Lorna was from Wyoming and had never seen the ocean, she said. Once, when Lorna found Jordan crying, she said tears were drops from the river of Heaven, whatever that was supposed to mean.

Three, Sandy, the bartender. His right hand had only three fingers. An accident with a skill saw when he'd had one too many. *Too many, two few, get it?* It didn't slow him down one bit. He made a mean margarita, Jordan's favorite. Once, when she was done for the night, she leaned on the bar, which was made of a single plank of fir, and told him she hated her life. "Lots of things you can hate in this world, but not life," he said. She had so much to drink, he told her to come home with him and sleep on the couch, as she hoped he would. Grandpa was being particularly difficult at that point, and she needed some time off.

Four, and last, Trevor, no longer on-again-off-again after he heard about Dwayne. His final text message to Jordan said, "Good luck. You'll need it."

As Jordan listened to Dwayne talking to Grandpa in that run-down excuse of a living room, she experienced a savage twinge of regret. She'd had those twinges before, many times. She knew it would pass quickly enough.

Five days later, on a back porch at the Lodge as the fire smoke swallowed the daylight and stung their eyes, Dwayne put his arm around her. She tensed. She'd kept to herself since their first night and wasn't used to him yet. He didn't sense it. He leaned in closer and gently brushed her hair from her face.

"You are a quiet little thing, aren't you?" he asked. He smelled of sweat. He'd been out on the trails all day with guests and hadn't showered yet. Jordan noted how much one man's sweat smelled like another. Grandpa wasn't the keenest bather, and he was often ripe.

She shrugged in response.

"See what I mean?" he asked. He kissed her. "Not that I mind, see. A talky woman can get on your nerves."

"That would be a tragedy."

"Did I do something to tick you off?"

She shook her head.

They sat and smelled the smoke.

A siren sounded from far down the valley.

"Another evacuation," Jordan said.

"Probably."

"Where are they going to go?"

"Dunno. Wenatchee, I guess. Maybe as far as Yakima."

Indian names, as if naming a town after a tribe could make up for anything.

"You know, you should get your granddad packed up, just in case," Dwayne said.

"He won't go."

"Might not have a choice. Police have the authority to move anyone out of the way, if they deem it necessary."

Jordan could tell how much Dwayne enjoyed using these official sounding words. Maybe he'd practiced them in front of a mirror. Once again, she scolded herself for not being fair.

You're a hard one, Miss Jordan. Which teacher had said that? Someone left over from the old days, who didn't believe in unnecessary kindness.

"You'll need to set him a good example," Dwayne said. "If you like, I can help."

"Help what? Pack?"

"Sure."

"You don't need to do that."

"Look, I know you're just putting on a brave

front."

"What do you mean?"

"With your granddad. Trying to cover for him, you know."

"No, I don't know."

"His mind. He's not all there."

"Oh."

"You're probably used to it. But I couldn't miss it for the world."

Jordan grew uneasy. She flexed her toes inside the tips of her comfortable black shoes. She'd had to buy them herself. The Lodge had supplied the uniforms the wait staff wore, a blue top and khaki pants for breakfast and lunch, and black shirts and black pants for dinner.

"What did he say?" Jordan asked, after another minute. The air was thickening.

"Stuff that just didn't make any sense."

"Like what?"

"Like what you're like in bed."

The sound of someone crying in the kitchen reached them. Probably Adele. She was a sous chef and had boyfriend problems.

"I knew he was talking about his wife. She died a while back, right?" Dwayne asked. His arm was still around her.

Jordan edged out of his embrace and stood. She held onto the smooth wooden railing, hoping to meet a splinter or a notch. Dwayne continued to sit.

"Anything else?" Jordan asked.

"Huh? You mean your granddad? Oh, the usual nutty stuff. He said Nixon was doing a great job."

A few moments before, Mount Robinson had been visible. Now it was gone. The smoke was coming closer. To her left, Jordan could see it flowing into the valley and up the opposite rise where her house was.

"Look!" Dwayne was on his feet. Flames had topped the rise from the other side. They were orange, not yellow, as Jordan thought they'd be.

It's time, she thought.

Barry Johnson, the Lodge's manager, called up to them from the outside landing.

"We're closing up! Best get a move on!"

Dwayne and Jordan went down the stairs. Dwayne offered to drive Jordan home, and stay until she and Grandpa were on their way to Wenatchee. Jordan said she didn't want to leave her car at the Lodge.

"I'll follow you, then," Dwayne said.

"What about your place? You better go get yourself cleared out."

He nodded. She could see that he hadn't really thought about that. His devotion to her was astonishing. Also annoying. *He's just trying to latch on. Probably can't stand being alone,* she thought, although she had no specific reason for believing so.

He followed her down the winding road from the Lodge, then turned left at the stop sign. Her house was to the right. When she arrived, Grandpa was at the kitchen table, working his way through a bottle of whiskey.

"Know what that imbecile told me? That we had to go. Damn fool. Still wet behind the ears, that one," he said. Jordan thought he was probably referring to the new sheriff's deputy, Matt Finch. He was a year younger than Jordan. They'd been in school together.

"He's just doing his job," Jordan said.

"As if there's any way I'm gonna leave the house I built with my own two hands and let it burn."

"Nothing you can do, Grandpa." Jordan knew for a fact that the house had been standing when Grandpa bought it.

"The hell you say."

Grandpa poured himself another drink and lit a cigarette. A siren sounded further down their road, sped past their property, and went on, distorted and elongated. Grandpa put his cigarette on the corner of his glass ashtray and missed. The cigarette rolled onto the table. She put the cigarette in the ashtray. It stayed this time.

He went on grumbling. She found his vial of sleeping tablets in the medicine cabinet, prescribed at her request during a phase when he was particularly active and bothersome at night. She dissolved four of them into a fresh glass of whiskey and gave it to him. He drank from it willingly. Twenty minutes later, his head was resting on the table. He snored. She packed her things. She had little. She included a photograph of her parents. She did not include a necklace Grandpa had bought her for her birthday some years before. She thought about stripping her bed, then decided that the flames, when they came, would do away with the whole structure.

The place where he'd taken her against her will, her frozen silence signaling acceptance. Which it was, really, when you didn't fight back, or struggle, or utter a single sound.

But fire made noise. It whooshed, and sighed, like an old man gone in the head and a girl desperate with loneliness and self-hate.

Well, this is what it all came down to. A pile of ash where a nightmare once stood.

She'd have to line things up, though. They'd want to know why she left without him.

He told me to go. He saw that I was afraid. He said

he'd be right along.

And you didn't argue. You just went.

I never argue with my grandpa. I wasn't raised that way.

And then there'd be a pause, time to consider the situation. Grandpa's mental state might come up.

Your sense of obedience is admirable. Yet the fact remains that you left an old man with memory problems alone in the path of a fire. Didn't you think he might get confused and not know what to do?

He wasn't confused at all. He was very clear. He told me to go and be safe.

Then she'd cry to demonstrate the depth of her loss. She'd offer the hope that he did make it somehow, and just hadn't checked in.

The burned-out shell of his truck was there. It's not likely he left on foot.

Maybe someone came and got him. Maybe—oh, I don't know!

Or perhaps none of this would happen, because the fire would take everything out, the valley and the hills and anyone who would ask questions. Maybe they would all be gone.

Only she would be left to stand on the beach for the first time in her life and watch small stones roll in the surf, where the wind lifting her hair was fresh and strong, and carried the smell of water and salt, not smoke.

where love lies

They were a common sight, the little white dog and the man who held his leash. They never rushed. On warm days they sat in the sun. The man dozed with his head to his chest, and the little dog lay on the ground with its nose on its paws. When the weather turned harsh, they moved to the coffee shop and took the last booth. No one came by to say it was time to go or minded that he had only one cup. He was allowed to stay while the light died down.

Such was life on the island. One was accepted, sometimes indulged, yet people weren't particularly friendly. They regarded each other coolly. Kept you at arm's length. Dana didn't care. She wanted to be left alone. The town respected that. Even so, there was gossip shared at the bakery or the hardware store. She'd overheard comments about folks she later recognized. *Had another one of those quiet weekends*, was whispered about the guy who ushered your car on and off the ferry, which meant he stayed home and got smashed. *Heard she spent all last week off-island, with that friend of hers.* The woman who sorted mail at the post office had a boyfriend her husband knew about and didn't object to. Dana didn't know what was said about her, but she could guess. *Is that hair for real, do you think? Never saw such frizz.* Her hair was tightly kinked, like an African's. Yet she was as white as milk. Forbearers came over on the Mayflower. Some rogue gene, no doubt, a mutation put there just to make people wonder. People didn't really care about her hair, though. They'd talk about her situation. *Husband beat the tar out of her. That's why she ran away. He'll be out in a year. Couldn't take the chance of him landing right back on their old doorstep.* But no one had those details. Rather, they probably just said she was divorced or separated, which would be clear from the white mark left by her now absent wedding band. She simply wanted to start over in a quiet, peaceful place.

Was it *too* quiet there? Dana wondered. Sometimes. At heart she was a hustle-and-bustle girl. Sidewalks and storefronts stirred her more than open fields and water views. The noise of the city made her laugh and feel alive, especially what she was liable to overhear: *She's as crazy as a box of hair, I'm telling you,* and, *I'm not kidding, he bought another monkey.* Here, when people weren't gossiping, they kept to the essentials. *Do you have any more energy-saver sixty-watt bulbs? Your tulips are looking lovely, aren't they?* Hardly conversation as Dana was used to having it. Politics had been the usual topic. The scoundrel Republicans lambasted at leisure over single-malt scotch. Chip always knew what should be done and how. She respected his expertise. He read history, political theory, and economics. Really, all they had to do was ask him.

He was tall, slender, and light on his feet. When he made a point, he did a jaunty two-step, like a rapid hop, one foot to the other. Then Chip lost his sense of humor. Sarcasm turned to rage, aimed not at the world in general, but at her. He thought Dana was lazy and useless. "Soft" was his favorite insult. Dana wasn't soft. She simply had never been poor, never had to bounce a check or eat Ramen for two weeks straight. Chip felt these things made him who he was, a superior person who really understood life. Dana didn't see it that way. She worked hard, didn't she? *At what? Those stupid paintings?* That hurt more than the slap which quickly followed. He didn't work at all, for money or for himself. Maybe that was the problem. Maybe he needed to find something to hang onto and give him self-esteem. "Cut the crap," he told her when she'd suggested exactly that. The apartment was hers. So was what they lived on. Well, it was her parents. They could afford to be generous. Chip hated them for having money. She told him if it bothered him so much, he should get a job. That earned another slap. She told him there wouldn't be a third, and to get the hell out. He broke her nose. She called the police.

There on the island, her work took on darker tones and ragged shapes. She never liked the idea of using art to work through personal problems—it seemed self-indulgent. Now she knew there was no choice—that what was inside of her would express itself, no matter what. Just as Chip's rage expressed itself. His love, too, even in those last, awful days. He held her while her nose bled. He wept with her. He was still crying when the officers snapped the cuffs on.

That was almost a year ago. She stayed in the city for a while. Her family urged her to leave and start over somewhere else. She went because she was sick of where she was, not because she was afraid Chip might find her one day. If he did, and tried to hurt her again, she would kill him. She believed herself capable of it.

The man with the dog, it turned out, also painted. They met in the art supplies aisle of the island's only hardware store, next to the home-ware section with its cheap, blue-speckled pots and pans. More suited to cooking on an open camp fire than on a six-burner gas range, Dana thought. Not that her small rental house had a six-burner range. It had a two-burner electric cook-top. On which she brewed the man, Bruce, a cup of herbal tea. He'd asked for coffee, which she didn't have. Nor sugar.

"Sort of a Spartan life you have going here, isn't it?" he asked her. He had the sharp, clear eyes of a young man, which surprised her. He wore a silver band with a dull green stone on one finger. His nails were short and dirty. The fingers were thick and scarred, more like a carpenter's than a painter's.

"Luxurious in its way," she said. Her home had a large room with a kitchen at one end and a wall of windows at the other. Her easel was set up by the windows, which faced due north. She slept in the upstairs loft, accessible by a narrow, poorly built wooden ladder that tended to shudder under her weight, though she was slim and slight. It suited her well. She adored it, in fact.

"A, 'less is more kind of thing'," Bruce said, staring into his tea. The top of his head was bald. His work confused her. There were lots of colored dots, in no order and suggesting nothing. He said that's how he saw atoms. Dana nodded. At that point, she was in his studio—his territory, after all, and who was she to disagree, though in truth she had to think that the universe was a bit more ordered than Bruce depicted it. It was people who disordered the universe with envy and rage. And grief. Grief caused the biggest wreck of all.

Bruce took up painting after his wife died. His home was large, well-furnished, and very comfortable. He painted in a downstairs room with only a small window, as if fighting distraction. The kitchen looked into the back garden that still had bright geraniums in pots, though it was late October.

The dog's name was Edgar, Dana assumed after Poe and didn't ask. Later, Bruce said his brother had been named Edgar, and he had been gone many years by then. Bruce was clearly lonely in a way Dana wasn't. He was sixty-three—thirty years her senior—yet she found him easier to be with than people her own age. He stopped in often. He liked to sit and watch her paint, and she didn't mind. Until he put his hand on her shoulder.

"Don't," she said.

"I'm sorry. It's just that you're a lovely woman."

Her eyes were her best feature, large and blue, but her nose was crooked, even before the break, and her chin a bit too prominent.

She got up, wiped her paint brush, and studied the scene she'd been trying—without success—to capture. Waves on rock. Something always in motion against something that never moved. She wanted to speed up time, show the process of erosion. On one side of the canvas, the rock was jagged and hard. On the opposite side, it softened, melted away. It was either brilliant, or inane.

"He must have hurt you real bad," he said.

66

"Who?"

"The one you ran away from."

She looked at her canvas again. Bruce went on looking at her.

"Am I wrong?" he asked.

Later that afternoon, at the Lower Tavern, she told him he wasn't wrong. But she also didn't want to talk about it, and he needed to respect that. He saluted her. He'd had a lot to drink. So had she. They each wondered if they'd end up in bed together. He was worried about it, and didn't let on. He knew what he felt for her would lead nowhere. Close companionship was the best he could hope for. He suffered from erectile dysfunction, and had for years. His wife had struggled to accept it, and often couldn't. She stepped out. He couldn't really blame her. Others did, because they didn't know what drove her. He was pitied for being cheated on. That pity was worse than the pain of her infidelity.

"Do you know what it's like to sit in a room with people who feel sorry for you?" he asked. His nose was red. There was a small splotch of bright blue paint on his cheek.

"No."

"You end up hating them."

"Hating's easy."

A truth she'd recently discovered. Hating was far easier than loving, and came more naturally, she thought.

"Living with it's not," Bruce said. That was true, too. So much truth. So much sharp, brilliant, blinding truth.

"Whoa," she said. She was wobbly, there on the barstool. He told her to take it easy. Then he said he loved her work.

"Really?"

"Indeed."

"You're the first person to."

"Don't believe it."

"Truth."

"Not one art teacher? Your folks? Even the ex?"

She shook her head. Her kinked hair swayed. One end of her silk scarf lay on the bar, close to a tiny puddle of beer. Painting was something no one else seemed to understand. Her painting, that is. She didn't understand it, herself. That was the problem. Basically, she saw the how, but not the why.

"Why?" she asked.

"What?"

"Do we paint."

Bruce shrugged. His shoulders were huge inside his worn flannel shirt. Chip's shoulders were narrow.

Maybe that's why he hit her—to prove that they weren't.

"No choice," Bruce said.

"What?" The music in the bar came up. Two people were dancing in a corner, their boots slamming the worn wooden floor.

"To paint. We got no choice but to."

"But to."

They thought about painting. Then they thought about lost loves. Dana figured nothing had been her fault. Bruce figured everything had been his fault. His head swam. He looked at her, slung low over her beer. She was a little thing. Like his wife. Sometimes he imagined her remains. The dried, curling flesh dressing the bones. And the smell of rot. Sometimes Dana imagined a different ending. Instead of sitting on the floor weeping, she threw the lamp at him. Then Chip was the one to cower and cry.

Winter was on the way. The annual holiday festival was held in the Odd Fellows hall, a converted barn that sat on a rocky cliff over the sea. Every year, Bruce was put in charge of decorating the inside, on the grounds that he was artistic and therefore had good taste. And he'd lived on the island for over twenty years. His tragedy was well-known and led him to be respected. Dana, as a newcomer, was allowed only a minor role. She was to stand and serve spiced cider. These decisions were made by Mary and Margaret Dykman: twins, widows, and owners of the island's knitting and crafts shop. They were short and squat, like a pair of soup cans. Their hands were fat and clumsy, and it was hard to see them handling the gorgeous yarn they sold. Dana had bought some her first week on the island, just because she loved the color—somewhere between plum and purple. The women asked her what she intended to do with the yarn. She didn't know. For a moment it seemed as if they might refuse to sell it to her.

"Maybe I'll use it to strangle someone," Dana had said.

Bruce hung tapestries stitched with sunflowers, and set out bright yellow tablecloths. They were cheerful, but didn't really evoke the holidays. Then someone mentioned that everything belonged to his late wife from some event she'd sponsored before ever coming to the island. It was Bruce's way of honoring her, one woman said in a hushed voice, as she took a cup of cider from Dana, then poured liquor into it from a tarnished silver flask she had in her plaid, wool coat.

There were a few children at the event, taking turns sitting on the knee of the man who ran the hardware store, Amos Rind. Amos wore an old, worn, and too-tight Santa suit. Watching him with the children, Dana wondered what it was like, growing up there. Her own childhood in the suburbs was easy and comfortable. She didn't remember visiting Santa, though, probably because her parents had never supported the myth of his existence. They were blunt, plain-spoken people—a trait which let her father, a cardiologist, earn the trust of his many patients and a good deal of money, too, which he invested in real estate in Suffolk County, on Long Island. Her mother, like the Dykman sisters, ran the small community they lived in, but out of the country club, not a crafts shop. Where other women kept their opinions quiet, Dana's mother never did. Yet she was well-liked, despite her painful candor. Even Chip liked her. *She tells it like it is.* Then he didn't like her. *She looks at me like I'm dirt.* That, after it became clear that he had no interest in getting a job, or going to school, or volunteering his time in some worthy cause.

"He acts as if it takes all of his energy just to wake up every day," her mother had said.

She was right about that.

"Having fun?" Bruce asked her. He had Edgar in his arms.

"Sure."

"I was watching you from over there. You're a

million miles away."

Dana wore a light blue sweater that matched her eyes, and a lapis pendant. He thought she looked nice, she could tell.

"Swing by on your way home. We'll have a drink," he said.

"Only one."

"Two at the most."

"Okay."

A scrawny young guy that Dana had seen in town a number of times, she thought his name might be Roy, plunked out "Silent Night" on the upright piano. Soon, an off-key crowd gathered around him. Dana watched the sky through the huge windows. Every building out there seemed to have a lot of glass. *Oh, holy night, the stars are...* and they were. She could see them clearly. She went to the window, drawn by their glitter. Was she sad? Maybe. She couldn't tell, because she'd forgotten how to feel. With the passing of time, even anger and the thrill of murder had grown cold.

The door opened, and the sudden wind sent dead leaves rushing over the floor. The man wore an old Army jacket and blue jeans. He carried a cardboard box full of candy canes, each individually wrapped in plastic. Dana could make them out clearly from the little distance between her and him. He wore a ponytail, streaked with gray. The stubble on his chin was both black and white. The eyes were piercing, the nose perfectly straight. He handed the box to one of the Dykman sisters, then stood briefly with his hands in the deep pockets of his jacket, then he made his way toward the punch bowl Dana had served from. He helped himself and looked around. When he saw her, he walked over. He didn't smile.

"Jesse," he said. His handshake was firm and his palm rough.

"Dana."

He nodded. His silence was unnerving.

"You must not live near town. I haven't seen you before," she said.

"I'm on the far side."

"Of the moon?"

"It can seem like it. Have you ever been out that way?"

"I don't think so."

Dana's exploration of the island was limited to the road that ran between her house, town, and Bruce's. She'd never gone anywhere else on the assumption that it would all look more or less the same. She didn't explain this to Jesse. He seemed to understand it, from the way he appraised her. Yet he didn't give an impression of being judgmental or unkind. Just knowing. The music stopped. Then another carol was underway. *Joy to the world* ... A baby cried. Someone coughed. Bits of conversation reached them. *It's true, they're orange ... That son of his is just no good ... Did you see that dress of hers? Heavens!* Edgar trotted past, chased by a little girl in a red dress and white tights.

"Come out sometime; I'll show you around," Jess said.

"I'll think about it."

He gave her directions.

Four days later, Bruce said he was sorry he missed her after the festival. She never stopped by. Meeting Jesse had rattled her—so much, in fact, that she hadn't gotten up the nerve to visit him yet, either.

"I'm sorry. I hope you didn't wait all night for me," Dana said. They were at her place. She'd been cleaning when he arrived. Sweeping the floor was soothing and let her mind wander to the far side of the island. Now Edgar lay under the table by Bruce's feet, dropping white hair on the dark planking.

"Not at all. I turned in early." He'd refused her offer of tea and was drinking from a bottle of wine he'd brought. It was early afternoon. She decided to join him. He said he hoped she was ready to put her heart on the line.

"I just met him. You act as if I'm madly in love,"

Dana said.

Bruce looked at her closely.

"One, I admit that it's none of my beeswax whether you take up with the fellow or not. Two, I think you probably will because, three, he's got a way with the ladies, and four, you should trust me on that one."

His tone was bitter. And sad. Dana had never heard him so sad. She put her hand on his.

"Tell me," she said, though she didn't really want to hear. It was what people did in a situation like that, though, wasn't it? Listen?

"He knew my wife."

"Oh."

"She had quite a thing for him."

"And he took advantage."

"On the contrary. He turned her down."

The wind came up. Snow was forecast for that evening, yet the sky was perfectly clear. Dana's place was heated with an enamel woodstove. It worked well. Sometimes it got too warm, and she opened a window. The air always smelled pure. City air never smelled like that. She loved living on the island, she realized. She wanted to stay.

She poured Bruce more wine. His face was heavy. He hadn't shaved. He didn't look rugged, but worn out.

"Go on," Dana said.

"He wouldn't reconsider. She couldn't take it, so she killed herself."

"My God!"

"You didn't know?"

"How would I?"

"You've seen how people up here talk."

"Not to me, they don't."

Bruce looked her in the eye. His expression softened. A sweet sentiment seemed to fill him up.

"That hair of yours," he said. Then he touched it. She leaned back. He withdrew his hand.

"When did all this happen?" she asked.

"Long time ago."

"I'm sorry."

Bruce nodded. She could see how hard it was for him to remember.

"Why didn't you move away?" she asked.

"Can't escape a thing like that, no matter where you go."

Edgar whimpered in his sleep.

"And there was no need, really. Jesse and I don't exactly cross paths, with him over there."

"What's he do?"

"Raises sheep. Sells their wool. Lives more or less like a hermit."

"How did your wife meet him?"

"She was a fiber artist."

"I see."

She got another bottle of wine, one she bought thinking she might drink it with Jesse. She put the bottle on the table, then she went to the window. The water was cut with whitecaps. A small motorboat with a cheerful yellow flag made its way into the wind. Gulls were lifted high on the gust, circled, and sank back to earth. Madrone trees leaned over the tall, rocky banks. Their bark shed naturally, exposing a deep red wood underneath. Dana wanted to paint them. She was done with dark seascapes. She returned to the table and opened the wine.

"He's a cold man," Bruce said.

"Cold?"

"The way he turned her down. Made her miserable. Awful to see."

"You wanted her to sleep with him?"

"No, of course not." He drank his wine. "I just didn't want her to get hurt."

"What was her name?"

"Lily."

A car came up the one-lane road. Its motor

struggled on the slope with an urgent, jerky whine. Bruce turned his head that way. Dana didn't. He turned back to her. His eyes were different now. They looked empty. She told him to take a little nap before heading home. The blanket she threw over him came from her grandmother, a simple weave of blue and white—nautical you might say—clean, antiseptic almost. Though he was a large man, the way he huddled beneath it made him look like a little boy.

A week later, with the island dusted in snow, Dana drove to Jesse's. She had a thermos full of hot cider, better than what was served at the festival. She thought to offer it to him as an apology for not showing up before. She could say she forgot, or was too busy, but he didn't ask what kept her.

He was in the barn with his sheep. He listed their names, but she wasn't listening. She watched his fingers as he stroked their heads in turn. They accepted his caresses blandly and ate the hay at their feet.

His house was cozy, with windows so old the glass was wavy. The wood floors creaked as they walked. The downstairs had a living room with full bookshelves. Books were stacked on the floor and on the kitchen table, too. The upstairs was one large room. The bathroom closed off at the far end. A skylight over the king-sized bed let in a broad swath of afternoon sunlight. On the table by the bed was a novel by Virginia Woolf. Dana asked where he got his books. He'd brought them to the island when he moved there. She didn't ask from where, or how long ago that was. He was good with his hands, she could tell. He'd refinished the stairs, balusters, and rail himself. He had plans to build an enclosed porch in back where he could sit in all weather and watch the sky. She said that sounded nice. He said he hoped she'd be willing to join him. They made love that evening.

Later, she told him she had never fallen in love with anyone so fast before. He said he loved her the moment he saw her.

"At the festival," she said. Their heads were on the same pillow.

"No. I saw you in town, walking with Bruce."

"You did?"

"Sure. More than once."

The night was full of stars. It was cold, and they made her think of ice. The warmth from the stove down below rose pleasantly. The room was comfortable. She told him about Chip. He listened, his face still. She waited for him to tell her about Bruce's wife. When he didn't, she prompted him.

"She was desperate. I don't know why she set her sights on me," he said.

"Come on."

"I'm nothing special."

Bull, she thought.

He was from Vermont, and moved west because he wanted a bigger sky to look at. On the island, there is nothing but sky, if you just kept looking up, he said. Or sea, if your gaze happens to fall. And in between, the deep, rich forest. Had she ever walked around in it? She said no, not yet. He'd take her when the weather improved, unless she didn't mind the cold. He wanted her to know that he wasn't always easy to be with. But he was consistent, dependable. He always showed up.

"How did she kill herself?" Dana asked.

"Gunshot. Opened her mouth and put it right in."

"How long ago was this?"

"Good eight, nine years."

Dana pulled the quilt tightly around her shoulders. It was an antique Desert Rose, from around 1900, that had belonged to his great grandmother. The quilt was thin and worn, though its reds and pinks were still bold.

On New Year's Eve, another snow was forecast, and Dana told Jesse to spend the night at her place. She was afraid the road would be bad for a while, and they wouldn't be able to see each other. She was also working on something she didn't want to leave, an abstract with pale colors within bold outlines, meant to suggest soft interiors and hard exteriors. He agreed.

She was at her easel when Bruce drove up. Jesse was on the couch with a book. Dana hadn't seen Bruce for a while. She'd found and not answered a note he'd left on her door asking her to have Christmas dinner with him. She felt guilty when she saw his face in the glare of the outside light. He asked her to put her brush away. He thought she might be more comfortable if she joined Jesse on the couch. Jesse got to his feet when Bruce came in, and Bruce told him to sit back down. His tone was flat. Edgar wasn't with him, Dana realized, and she wondered if he'd come to say that he'd died. He sat at Dana's table. She offered him a drink, and he refused. He talked about Lily, how New Year's was her favorite holiday. It always perked her up, the idea of starting over. Dana said in that case she was glad Bruce decided to spend it with them. She became aware of Jesse beside her on the couch, of the shift in his position. He leaned forward with his elbows on his knees.

Bruce put the gun on the table. It caught the light from the fireplace. Its handle was heavy and blunt-looking. Dana had never seen a gun in person before. She'd thought of taking shooting lessons after Chip, and then didn't.

"Why couldn't you love her?" Bruce asked. "That's all she wanted. All she needed. She'd be here now, if you hadn't turned her down."

Jesse stood up and asked Bruce to leave. Bruce stared at the floor. Then Dana stood up, too, and came toward Bruce. Bruce picked up the gun and pointed it at her. Then he aimed it at Jesse.

"This is the second woman you've stolen from me. Don't you think that's enough?" Bruce asked. Jesse said something Dana didn't comprehend. She was looking at the gun. Suddenly, it was the only thing in the room.

Afterwards, the people on the island couldn't stop talking about what had happened. But then, as always, their enthusiasm faded, and life went on. Waves washed the rocky shore, fields greened and then turned brown, the sky opened and closed like a secret briefly shared. Every now and then, though, someone would remember and consider, just for a moment, where love lies.

the keeper of the truth

The crystals in the window would have thrown a rainbow in the sun. The sun wasn't out, though. It was winter, and the world was gray. The woman was gray, too, and not just her hair, but her suit, with a small pin in the shape of a seahorse angled on the right lapel. She didn't go by Madame Zolara or any sort of exotic name that conjured an intimacy with the spirits, but by Gwen. *Psychic Gwen.* Painted in gold, loopy letters across the dusty glass door.

Emily was there for research. She was writing a book on soothsayers, visionaries, and fortune tellers. Women with gifts, women beyond the mainstream and how they had been perceived, and treated, over time. She'd done enough reading, and needed a primary source, so had driven up South Hill in the snow, struggling to find the right address among the storefronts whose numbers had faded or disappeared.

Psychic Gwen gestured to a folding metal chair by a small, round table. Emily sat down, and Psychic Gwen took the chair opposite her. Emily didn't know what to do next. The last time she had interviewed anyone was back in high school when she'd worked for the local newspaper as an intern. The person they'd matched her up with was a local politician, a Second Ward alderman, a crusty old Irish Catholic who talked about "bad elements" moving to Dunston, then offered her a cigarette.

After a moment, while Psychic Gwen held Emily's gaze in a way that made her uneasy, she said, "There are some things I'd like to ask you." It was a short list: *When did you first suspect that you were psychic? Did you tell anyone? If so, what was the reaction?*

Psychic Gwen reached across the red velvet tablecloth and took Emily's hand. She gazed into the palm which had suddenly dampened with sweat, then turned it a little toward the only source of light in the room, a small lamp on top of a large and very dusty roll-top desk.

"You will live a long life," Psychic Gwen said. "Much of it alone, but not all." She peered more closely. "You will not have children, yet there was a child once."

At twenty-two Emily had an abortion. Her boyfriend was in love with someone else, needing Emily for comfort until his true love took him away. Emily never told him about the baby. She never told anyone.

Emily reclaimed her hand.

"Please. There are things I want to ask," she said.

Psychic Gwen took out a deck of Tarot cards from a drawer on her side of the table. She spread them out, face down, with the skill of a Las Vegas dealer.

"The cards hold all your answers. Point to one," Psychic Gwen said.

Emily sighed. This was a bad idea, she now saw. She pointed to a card.

"The Chariot," Psychic Gwen said. "This means you desire to exert control and find it difficult to do so. Now, choose again."

Emily pointed to a second card.

"The Hanged Man. You want to let something go, change direction, reverse your fortune. These cards are in opposition, as are you, torn between two objectives, unsure of the outcome. The third card will decide your fate."

Emily's third choice was the Ten of Swords. "You feel like a victim, on the receiving end of another's folly. You have put this person's welfare above your own."

Psychic Gwen put the cards back in the drawer and told Emily she had a stain on her soul.

"You have carried it there a long time. Yet one day, you may wash it clean."

Emily gave up on the questions she'd prepared and handed Gwen the twenty-dollar bill she'd been asked to pay when she made the appointment on the phone, refused a receipt, and rose to go.

"I will see you again," Psychic Gwen said. At those rates, Emily didn't think that likely.

The snow fell harder. What had taken over thirty minutes to get to Psychic Gwen's became over an hour to return home—to the house she had taken possession of from her mother and father when they moved to Arizona. They hoped to put it on the market within the year and counted on Emily to supervise the sale. She lived there rent-free because at the time the arrangement was made, she was in school, plugging away on her doctoral thesis. Her parents assumed she still was. Emily had withdrawn from the university the previous autumn after the man she was having an affair with went back to his wife. At that point, school became too much.

She kept on with the project though, the book. Several weeks after seeing Gwen, she changed focus. Psychics were interesting (and unnerving, she had learned), but she wanted a wider subject, to emphasize current thinking about aberrant behavior and then say how society had changed its mind over time about why people did what they did. Witches were just people who didn't fit in, didn't do what the world expected of them. Today those witches would be labeled with low self-esteem or attention deficit disorder, be obsessive-compulsive, have an addictive personality, have repressed memories only the most skilled therapist could uncover. People weren't evil anymore, they were afflicted, subject to a cure given the right tools, the right environment, and a guiding hand.

Emily explained this to her friend Lisa over a shared six-pack of beer, imprudently consumed on an empty stomach.

"You know why you're so into this, right?" Lisa asked.

"Because I want to know about the human psyche. The *soul*."

"No one knows anything about the soul. Except when it hurts."

"Or has a stain."

Lisa stared at Emily, then burped with the gusto of a seasoned drinker.

"The psychic told me my soul has a stain," Emily said.

"Yeah, and its name is Melissa."

Emily's sister wasn't exactly a stain, Emily thought, though she'd definitely left her mark on the members of her family.

*

Two days later, Melissa showed up in the middle of

the night from Boston, carrying all her possessions in one large backpack. Things had dried up on her there. Her contacts had moved on, and with one arrest for possession four years before, she didn't want to chance anyone new, some zealous undercover cop, maybe, out to climb the departmental ladder. She hadn't been back two days when the calls started. Old friends, deadbeats wanting to hook up and get high, and people she hadn't seen in years showed up at all hours, woozy and smiling, or sullen, strung out, wanting to sleep on the couch.

Emily stayed out of their way. She was raised on tiptoeing around. Also on the theory of redemption. One morning, when Melissa got up before noon, Emily asked, "What about What's-his-name? Tom? Why don't you give him a call?"

"No fucking way."

Tom was someone Melissa had slept with on and off for years. He'd already offered her a bed at his place, but Melissa knew better. He had a bad habit of trying to rehabilitate her. He didn't give her money, because he'd done that before, money for food and some classes at the community college that she put up her nose. Staying with him meant a lecture on free will and right choices, all the bullshit she'd heard forever.

As if sensing her return, their parents called one

night. She was out again, and Emily was free to fill them in. They made nice noises. *That must be hard for you,* and, *You're so good to help out.* The baton had been passed. Melissa couldn't be abandoned. They just couldn't turn their backs. A hand had always been extended, and always would be. They sent money. Emily took her share above living expenses. She was building a little bank account. As for the rest, Melissa would need new clothes—nothing expensive, just basic, practical. Jeans, shoes, underwear. Their mother was keen on new underwear. Emily would do the buying. Melissa was not to be trusted with cash. Or valuables, either, for that matter. Two years before, Melissa had pawned their grandmother's diamond brooch. The five thousand dollars kept her and her most recent boyfriend in pot and booze for two weeks in a Vegas hotel suite. Their mother's face stayed hard for a month. Their father retreated behind the closed door of his study. The time for threats and rebukes had ended years earlier, after Melissa's second arrest for drunken driving.

The judge assigned her to substance abuse counseling. The sessions often involved a group. Melissa made friends easily with anyone who bought her a drink afterwards. Her parents put her in therapy, first with an older woman who lived on a farm and raised goats. She felt Melissa was responding to an unspecified childhood trauma. Then they sent her to a younger man who wore sweaters and pressed pants. Melissa tried to pull his heartstring. She wept through several sessions. He prescribed anti-depressants. She said she'd prefer Vicodin. He refused. She offered him oral sex. Again, he refused. She threatened to say he was the one who'd propositioned her. He gave her the prescription and told her never to come back. After that, the help of outsiders was no longer sought.

*

On a gray, freezing Tuesday, Emily awoke with a taste of doom. The silence of the world was both final, and fatal. Her mind's eye gave a scene of total destruction. She had had these dreams before. The lone survivor. The keeper of the truth.

And there he was on the couch, snoring. A man she didn't know. Her gentle nudge didn't rouse him. Her hard slap did.

"What the fuck?" he asked. He'd brought his dog, a leggy mutt with a bald patch who'd shit everywhere, then dug up Emily's rubber tree plant.

"Out," Emily said.

"She said she lived alone, man. Who the fuck are you?"

"Her mother."

He sat up. His eyes came into focus. "Yeah, right," he said.

Emily raised her hand once more.

"Jesus. You got any coffee?"

Emily gave him five dollars from her purse, took his backpack, and tossed it out the front door. The dog ran after it, and peed liberally on the first bush it came to.

Afterwards, she banged on Melissa's door until she answered. Melissa emerged. Her face was puffy and her breath stank. She looked at the mess and nodded. Emily dressed and escaped.

She thought of walking by the lake, but the wind was bitter so she went to a coffee shop and sat a long time. Melissa wasn't bad. She was just weak. As a child, Melissa could never resist temptation. She opened Christmas gifts early. She ate treats saved for guests. Emily, two years older, tried to correct her. They often fought. One time was particularly harsh. Their grandmother died suddenly when Melissa was six and Emily eight. Melissa said she knew it had happened when the phone call came. Their grandmother was healthy and strong. They'd seen her only a week before. Her death shocked them. But not Melissa, who swore she sensed it as her grandmother kissed her good-bye and went down the walk to her car. Emily said Melissa didn't know anything, that she invented the whole thing.

She went home. The house was clean. There was a vase of white carnations on the kitchen table, her favorite winter flower, and a card with a picture of a kitten and Melissa's words, *To new beginnings.*

Melissa came home late, drunk, eyes dilated, stinking of cigarette smoke and sex. Her attempt to move silently through the house was foiled by breaking a glass in the kitchen. Since she had removed her shoes trying not to make noise, the shards had cut the bottom of one foot, right through the thin socks she wore. Emily found her sitting on the floor, looking at her bloody sole, sobbing.

Emily helped her to bed. She thought the scope of her research had to include normal people affected by the spiritually lost. *We are like the light they fly to,* she wrote in her notebook, then crossed it out.

Two days later, Melissa forgot her key and banged on the door well after midnight. Emily was still up, trying to organize her thoughts. She'd resurrected the light idea. *We are the beacon that guides them home.* When Emily didn't answer, Melissa stood in the yard and shouted. Then she threw small pebbles at Emily's bedroom window. Emily peered through the crack in the curtains. Melissa had no coat. Emily sat another minute. She'd have to confirm if her theory were historically accurate. Had the visionaries had stable companions around them, people who helped them along? The idea of more research was both thrilling and tiresome. Emily was a good researcher, though. Of that she was sure.

When she opened the front door, Melissa said, "You hate me."

"Only the things you do."

Melissa went to bed. Emily realized that her book still lacked the proper focus and would never grab anyone's attention. The next day, she put her work away in a drawer, and left it there.

Spring came. The trees filled the blank spaces of winter sky with tiny, soft buds, and the air, still cool, was lovely and fresh. Melissa went to Florida with a college student she'd met in a bar, and Emily had the place to herself.

Her parents called again. They said there was no point in doing anything with the house while Melissa was still there. Emily was relieved. They asked how her work was going. She said it was coming along nicely.

Melissa returned. She was tanned and sober. She had new clothes. The college student seemed to have a little money. She didn't mention him, or say much of her time away. She wanted to make dinner for Emily. Emily didn't like the idea, but she consented.

Melissa was a decent cook, when she put her mind to it. She'd once talked of making a career in the kitchen, attending cooking school, even having her own restaurant one day. She asked Emily for thirty dollars to buy groceries with. Emily said she should make a list, and she'd shop, herself. Melissa said she didn't know what she was going to make yet. She'd take her inspiration from what looked good at the store. Emily hesitated. Melissa got upset.

"You don't trust me," she said.

"No, it's not that; it's just …"

"I know, I know. Can't you see I've changed, though?"

She did look different, Emily had to admit. She was clean and neat. Even her nails were free of dirt.

At seven-thirty that evening, Emily sat alone with a glass of wine. Melissa had been gone for hours. She hadn't called. Emily actually believed she would call. She hated herself for that.

The next morning, Melissa returned. She wasn't clean or neat. Her jacket was stained with mud, and her hair, tidy and clipped the day before, hung in her face. She'd been crying.

Emily sat her down and gave her a cup of coffee.

"He threw me out," Melissa said.

"The college kid?"

Melissa nodded. "He said his parents were coming up from the city, and I couldn't be there. He didn't want them to meet me."

"Did you want to?"

Melissa shrugged.

"It's just the principle of the thing, right?" said Emily.

Again, Melissa shrugged, but Emily knew she'd hit a nerve. Even Melissa, with all the harm she did others, didn't want to feel like a low life who wasn't good enough to meet someone's family.

"You can't expect people to treat you better than you act," said Emily.

"What the fuck is that supposed to mean?"

"You make bad choices. People get tired of it, and they move on."

"Yeah? Well, fuck them."

"Easy to say."

Melissa hung her head. She was still drunk, Emily could tell.

She looked around the dining room where they were sitting. The wallpaper had a pattern of daisies and bluebells. It was old, outdated, and ugly.

Melissa sneezed. "I think I'm getting sick," she said.

Emily put her hand on her forehead. "You feel

warm. Go take a shower and get into bed."

"Is there any wine in the house?"

"It's ten-thirty in the morning."

"Tell my head that."

Emily got her a glass of wine. Melissa's mood got better. She became expansive. She made fun of the college boy, said he was pudgy and too fast in bed. Emily laughed. Melissa's charm had always been like a crystal, throwing light here and there. Sometimes it fell on you, and you were a little brighter for a while, too.

Melissa showered, got into her pajamas, and let Emily tuck her in. She was soon asleep. Emily took the manuscript she'd hidden in her desk drawer, tossed into the fireplace, and lit it. A lot of her life turned to ash as she sat and watched. Maybe that was what she was best at—sitting and watching. It didn't really matter. There were no visionaries or special spirits or gifted hearts. Only people who broke the rules. And others who covered their nakedness, kept them safe, and loved them so blindly that they never grew up or improved in any way.

an act of concealment

In August, 1920, two newlyweds descended the stairs of the railroad car that had brought them to Huron, South Dakota. They took in the hot, flat landscape and realized at once that there was no lake. The husband, Paul Emile, had accepted the teaching position there because of the presence of a wide body of water which he would later learn was one of the Great Lakes, and considerably to the north and east of where he then stood with his wife, Anna. He had grown up on the shores of Lake Geneva. Living by water was necessary for serenity of spirit, he believed. Waiting for their taxi to take them into town, breathing the dry, dusty air, he thought the place he looked at was nothing like home. His heart sank a bit.

Anna's heart didn't. To her, home was an idea, not a place. The Turks had removed her family from their villa in Constantinople five years before. They were not forced out into the countryside to die as so many others were, because her father was a jeweler by trade and not considered any sort of political or ethnic threat, but into a far poorer neighborhood than they'd enjoyed before. The house they came to occupy was much smaller than the first, which had had a long stone balcony overlooking the Bosphorus where Anna played as a child and later sat as a young woman dreaming of lands that lay beyond her line of sight. In time, the only land she dreamed of was America, and she'd arrived. Now all there was to do was make the best of it.

They'd secured a cottage near the campus of Huron College. Whoever had lived there before had had a fondness for drink, judging from the whiskey bottles set neatly on the dusty windowsill. One bore the label *Uncle Oscar's Pick Me Up—A Tonic for Well-Bred Ladies.* Anna removed the cork and brought the open vessel to her nose. All she got was a faintly floral smell. The bottle was nicely shaped—slender at the neck, wider in the middle, and tapering again to the base on which it sat.

As she turned the bottle over in her hands, the tiny diamond in her wedding band flashed in the light. Theirs had been a Catholic ceremony, in a church on a narrow, quiet street. Paul so handsome in his long coat and combed-down hair. Only one of his five sisters made the trip south from Le Lac, the Swiss village of his birth. Anna had not met her before. Unlike her brother, she was short and thick, with a stubborn, sullen gleam in her brown eyes. Like a cow's, those eyes, Anna thought. Marie came to serve as Anna's maid of honor. It was not up to the bridegroom to choose who would fill that role, but Anna let him, to the pain and quiet sighs of her own two sisters. She let him do anything. She had waited a long time to draw a man's eye. She was thirty years old.

She brought the bottle into the kitchen and put it by the sink then lifted and pumped the iron handle until a stream of brown water flowed from the faucet. There was nothing to stop the sink with, so Anna released the pump. A list formed in her mind of things to buy in town, things she hoped the college would reimburse them for.

Paul had the same thought. He believed in counting pennies. The coat he'd worn at his wedding had been borrowed. Anna's ring belonged to his dead aunt, a fact he didn't share with her, though Marie obviously knew. He'd sworn her to silence telling her she was such a big help to him growing up, though in fact she hadn't been. Marie was five years older than he, unmarried, generally lazy. She served tea in a small establishment with pink and gold wallpaper that catered to better-off women in Geneva. She was also gullible, and susceptible to flattery. Anna wasn't. His praise and kind words were accepted without so much as a flicker in her black eyes. He loved those eyes. Her steel core made other means of persuasion necessary. Sex had proven to be the answer. He hoped Anna would soon be pregnant.

She continued her inspection of the house.

There were two bedrooms: the one in front faced east, the one in back faced west. There were no curtains in either room. The bathroom was next to the kitchen. The tile floor was missing here and there, and the mirror above the sink was cracked. Anna examined her reflection in the mismatched glass. Her face split just above her mouth, so that above the line she was herself, with no way to speak, and below, she was only words. *I'll have to figure out what that means later*, she thought, and then forgot all about it.

Paul went to campus every morning promptly at nine, although courses wouldn't begin for another week. He wanted to become well acquainted with everyone in the French Department. The Chairman had taken particular interest in Paul's doctoral thesis, written while he was an instructor at the American University in Constantinople where Anna was a secretary. The topic of Paul's dissertation was Denis Diderot and his philosophy of enlightenment. The Chairman, Donald Plake, had never been to France. His son had died during the Battle of the Somme. In Paul Emile he saw a second son, someone his own might have become given time and opportunity. Professor Emile was no doubt highly cultured, Professor Plake said during the staff meeting he'd held just hours before Professor Emile arrived in Huron. In person, Professor Emile exceeded

Professor Plake's expectations. All that old-world charm! The slight bow of greeting. The heels of his polished shoes always lined up side-by-side as he stood, absolutely straight. He'd won a medal for marksmanship, Professor Plake confided to his wife. And it was so easy to see him: his hand steady, nerves calm, not a drop of sweat on his brow.

In truth, Paul was given to bouts of melancholy that left him anything but steady and calm. He was a fearful man. He suffered from unnamed slights and insults, and took his misery out on Anna, sometimes refusing to speak, other times flying into a childish rage. Her own father had an uneasy temperament. She felt at home with his bad humor. She was willing to bide her time and wait for the episode to pass, which it always did, most quickly after a soothing cup of tea and a little story she shared from her own past.

Once, she'd lost a button from her favorite blouse. A small pearl button held in place with fine silk thread. After the move, with their money all but gone, replacing that button was impossible. The finery she once enjoyed glimmered for a moment in her eyes, though Paul, sunk in despair over the sudden laughter from one his students—and on his first day in the lecture hall, no less—didn't notice.

Anna's only choice was to find a fake pearl button, easy to come by in any notions store. The man who sold it to her said it matched the others perfectly. Anna, with her damaged shirt in hand, agreed.

"It'll be your secret," he said as he put the button in a paper bag. But Anna wasn't sure. Her mother had sharp eyes. So, she removed all the buttons and sewed the fake pearl at the bottom, where the shirt was usually tucked into the waistband of her ankle-length skirt.

Paul's spirits lifted a bit as Anna said her mother never knew a thing. He liked the idea of concealment. He lived on it, in fact.

He was nearly found out the first week in Huron, when their neighbor marched in, pie in hand, to welcome them. Paul and Anna were unpacking; the afternoon was quite warm, hence the open front door. The neighbor stopped by the sideboard and said she'd never seen a candelabra quite like that. Paul explained what it was used for.

"It belongs to my wife," he added.

Anna thought he was silly. It might have been important in Switzerland, or even in Constantinople, but out there, in the American West, who would care? Paul didn't relent. It had to be this way. He couldn't risk the college learning the truth and taking issue with it. He said that his family had always practiced in secret. To their friends and neighbors, they were strict Calvinists, which is what he'd indicated on his application for employment at the college.

So, the menorah became hers, and she the Jewess.

She passed on her deep olive complexion, black hair, and knowledge of Middle Eastern cuisine.

Sometimes she requested items from Mr. Norquist, the green grocer, that he didn't stock or even know. One such item was eggplant. She described it at length. Mr. Norquist turned red when she gave its size and the texture of its skin. He recovered himself by saying he didn't have goods just yet for the chosen people, but would see what he could do.

Another time she wanted grape leaves. "Must be another Jewish delicacy," he told her. Anna didn't mention that grape leaves were, in fact, used in a Greek dish called dolmas, because he wasn't being unkind, only ignorant. She wasn't mistreated, but regarded with curiosity, as an alien being.

She wasn't alone. There was a family: a husband, wife, and two boys. The husband repaired musical instruments. The wife painted miniature landscapes. One of their boys recited poetry; the other had a flair for baseball. She was often asked, "Do you know the Greenbergs?" When she said no, she was occasionally given directions to their home, as if she wanted nothing more than to connect with other Jews.

*

Her neighbor, Britta Lund, lived one block over. Their backyards faced off across an alley. After the pie, they met again while hanging laundry. Britta's red hair lay in a long braid down her broad back. She stood well over a head taller than Anna, but then everyone did. Anna barely topped five feet tall. She wore a size three shoe. These facts were later shared over a cup of strong coffee that Britta served in her spotless, stuffy kitchen. Britta explained that the window sash was broken.

"My husband got no time to fix it," she said with pride. Her husband, Lars, owned the town's hardware store. He'd just bought the property next door and was expanding. Anna patted the perspiration from her forehead with a lovely linen handkerchief she'd embroidered herself. Britta admired it.

"I'd ask my son, but he's under the weather," Britta said.

"I'm sorry to hear that."

"He needs his rest, Olaf does."

Britta's gaze wandered when she said this. She took in her entire kitchen, it seemed, and settled on her plump, red hands, folded in her lap. She sniffed.

Anna suspected that there were tears in her eyes. *Her son must be quite ill,* she thought. But no, because he was walking through the house just then, with a firm, strong tread. The front door opened and closed. Britta lifted her head. Her eyes were clear. She sighed. She looked relieved.

Anna was quick to deduce from what she overheard around town that Olaf, who'd been in the war, just wasn't the same since coming home. Once a lively, cheerful young man, after he came home he mostly kept to himself. Before enlisting, he was often seen behind the counter of the family store in a crisp white apron, weighing out nails and giving advice on saw blades. Now he was seldom in the store. Where he seemed to go most regularly was to the Lutheran church Paul attended, since the Calvinists weren't represented in Huron. Paul was a bit sorry about that. He'd gotten so used to their ways, but thought the Lutherans were just as good, really. Sometimes Anna went along. People said it was strange for a Jew to attend a Christian service, and speculated that perhaps Anna's husband was hoping she'd convert. When Anna heard that, she found it rich. She had begun to develop a cynical edge about the arrangement she'd had no choice but to accept; the edge was made sharper after learning about Olaf and the war, since Paul had sat out that same war on account of Switzerland's neutrality.

Olaf suffered from shell shock, but those words were not used. Like his mother's suggestion that he needed rest, other people spoke of him in terms of being overworked, exhausted, run thin. Anna couldn't believe that he was the only young war veteran in Huron who suffered thus, and in fact, he wasn't. The difference was that other soldiers had someone pulling them along—a sweetheart, for instance, a wife, sister, or mother. Always a female, Anna noticed. And since Olaf was unmarried and an only child, the only one who could fill that role for him was his own mother. Britta didn't want to interfere with his life, she said, in a moment of surprising candor once again over a laundry line.

"He will find his own way," she said firmly, pulling a pair of men's flannel underwear from the line and throwing them into her basket. She and Anna hadn't been talking about Olaf, but about the weather. Britta said that with the first cold snap they now felt on their cheeks, it wouldn't be long before the men would want to get out their cross-country skis and make sure they were ready for winter. When the snow fell hard, as it quite often did, Britta assured her, the only way to get around town was on skis. Olaf was a fine skier, she said. Once, as a young boy, he'd made his way all alone to a neighbor's out in the country to check on them after a blizzard. The family hadn't been seen in town and had no telephone. So, off Olaf went, before anyone could gear up and come along, too. The family needed medicine for their daughter, down with fever. They were in Olaf's debt to that day.

Olaf crept into whatever conversation his mother had sooner or later, Anna noticed. The husband, Lars, whom Anna had spoken to only at his hardware store when she'd gone first to buy picture wire to hang a portrait of her mother, then a new broom and dust pan, and lastly a rolling pin, didn't mention him at all. And in church, the father didn't sit with his wife and son, but off by himself as if embarrassed—even disgusted—by his son's frailty.

Soon Paul earned a reputation at the college for his teaching style and skill. He walked back and forth before the chalkboard, hands behind his back, head down, gazing at the dusty floor. His boots made tracks in that dust. His talk of man's rational mind made tracks in the hearts of those green farm boys— and a few farm girls.

Religion—and the fear of religion—is put aside!

Man must think for himself and find a reasoned balance, informed by the necessity of doing good—not for selfish motives, but only for practical gain.

The mind holds sway over all.

If they only knew that their professor was not himself a rational man! Anna couldn't help being bitter. She was lonely there in Huron. She missed her family. Her father had died some years before, and her mother sent imploring letters, begging her to come back. Anna replied that no return was possible and told her mother to have faith in the Virgin Mary. Anna's own faith was no stronger than before, yet sometimes she removed her rosary from the green alabaster box which had been her wedding gift from an uncle she'd never met, and said a few Hail Mary's. There was comfort in ritual, she discovered once more. Something Paul knew, too, given the peace, however temporary, that descended upon him after reading the Torah.

Professor Plake invited Paul and Anna to his home to celebrate Halloween. They had never celebrated Halloween. In Constantinople, the American University hosted a party every year, so they were familiar with the wearing of costumes. They recalled one young man who dressed as a bear and carried the head of his outfit under one arm when he got overheated. A woman in the style of Marie Antoinette lost her fancy wig in the fountain. Paul was nervous about attending the party. Groups made him uneasy. There were that many more chances to make a fool of oneself, he thought. He did so much better one-on-one. Anna said he should relax. He was doing very well. His students adored him. She'd heard nice things as she went about her errands in town. More smiles came her way, just for being his wife. She could see him trying to believe her.

On the day of the party, Paul took to his bed. He was sick, he said, though his forehead was cool. He refused to eat. Anna tempted him with roasted chicken, his favorite. Finally, he consented to take a bite. He propped himself up in bed and worried what would be thought of him for not coming to the party. Anna said she'd already called Professor Plake on the telephone.

"I told him you were indisposed. He was very sympathetic," she said.

"You shouldn't have done that."

"Why not?"

Paul didn't answer. Anna watched him struggle with himself over the lie she'd told on his behalf. Part of him was afraid of being found out. Another part was ashamed. He would not resolve the conflict, nor make peace with it. He would allow it to torment him until it was replaced by the next crisis.

She washed the dishes, alone in the kitchen. But did one allow oneself to be tormented by guilt, she wondered? Or was it the case that one simply couldn't avoid it? She never felt guilty, herself. She merely regretted certain deeds and circumstances. And hardness of the heart. *Intractability.* That was not one of Paul's character traits. It was one of hers, and she was sorry she possessed it. She hadn't always. She began life as tender-hearted as anyone. Yet at some point she became less kind. As a teenager, she saw the emotional cruelty her father inflicted on her mother. Then she saw what happened to her countrymen. Now she understood that her husband was a child, and rather than making her want to soothe and comfort him, she wanted to give him the back of her hand.

It's all right to get annoyed, she told herself. *You're still a good wife.*

A light was on in the Lund's kitchen. Olaf stood before the window gazing into the night. Anna shut off her own light, so he wouldn't see her there, gazing back. He poured himself a glass of water and didn't drink it. He gripped the counter. Anna could see how hard he was holding it from the way his shoulders pulled forward. He hung his head for a moment, as if it had become too heavy to bear. Then he released the counter, stood straight, and left the kitchen. A moment later, Britta appeared to wash out the glass, dry it, and put it in a cupboard. Her expression was grim. Anna knew how she felt. She also lived with an invalid.

"But you *must* come. We always have the neighbors for a small celebration," Britta said. The Christmas season was upon them. Candles burned in windows. Wreaths were nailed to doors—including Paul and Anna's—and a tree lot stood behind the courthouse with evergreens from as far away as Wisconsin. Neither Paul nor Anna had had a Christmas tree before. The idea was thrilling.

"I understand if you might feel out of place. But believe me, no one will care that you're not Christian," Britta said in a low voice, though they were alone in Anna's dining room, where the menorah sat on the sideboard with its burned down candles. Each night of Passover, Paul had made sure to have Anna draw the heavy curtains she'd made herself before he lit the candle and prayed.

"I can't imagine how I'll talk to them." Anna sipped her coffee. She was being wicked, and enjoyed it.

"My dear! You mustn't worry. You get on quite well with me, now don't you?" Britta wore a pin with a blue stone that complimented her round eyes nicely.

"All right then, I'll be glad to. I can't speak for my husband. He's often quite tired from teaching."

"But the college isn't in session? Surely, he could

rest up beforehand."

Britta was keen that they both come. Paul had earned himself a reputation for being charming and witty, a reputation that extended beyond his lecture hall. He was easily recognized in town, and sometimes people approached him to say how much their son or daughter was enjoying his course. Their words always brought his hand to the brim of his hat in recognition of the honor paid him. Women, especially, watched him as he came and went from campus to home on foot. He was a dashing, handsome man, there was no doubt. Anna wondered if she might find herself with a rival for his affection, then dismissed the idea at once.

As she had anticipated, Paul took to his bed again on the evening that they were due at the Lund's. She knew it was her duty to stay with him, yet she refused. He sulked. She said she couldn't let their neighbor down, that Britta was counting on her. Paul turned his face to the wall. Anna knew that she would pay later. He would refuse to speak to her for several days, communicating his needs only in writing. Then he would be contrite and buy her a little gift. These small, inexpensive tokens of apology were collected on her bureau. A white vase, a silver pendant, a paper fan. Buying so often, and always for his wife, further enhanced his stature in the town. What a wonderful husband! How kind and loving! Some speculated, not always in private, that Anna was demanding and required frequent presents to keep her satisfied. One woman, the baker's wife, not Scandinavian like so much of the town but a bulky Russian whose apron was always dirty, whispered to her husband that Jews were often that way.

Anna wore a red velvet dress she'd sewn herself with material she bought with leftover housekeeping money. Paul hadn't noticed her skimping; she was that skilled in the kitchen. She often bought day-old bread and used it as a crust over a pot of roasted chicken and vegetables the green grocery put on sale after two or three days. She spent a bit of money on dried spices, oregano and thyme, considered quite a luxury but necessary to disguise the bland taste of food on the edge of going bad. It was worth the risk. She'd known luxury once, long ago, and sometimes she just had to have it.

She pinned her luscious black hair with two large mother-of-pearl clips. She draped her amber bead necklace, strung on sturdy wire, not string, around her neck. Lastly, she fastened her mother's cameo to her left shoulder. She was elegant, and knew it. She didn't care if she put anyone to shame that night.

During her short walk, the falling snow collected

on her hair. She found the snow exhilarating. She had never seen it before, and stopped to observe how it floated and swirled around her.

Britta took Anna's coat quickly, almost roughly. There was trouble in the kitchen, she said. The dinner wasn't coming out quite right.

"I hate to do this to you, on a night like this, but I don't know who else I can ask."

Olaf stood at Britta's stove, mournfully basting a tired-looking turkey which sat in an oval pan. He lifted the ladle slowly and poured a greasy-looking broth over its pimply skin. He was dressed for the evening in a black coat and gray wool slacks. His blond hair was combed down flat. When Britta said his name, he turned and looked down at Anna with the most piercing blue eyes she had ever seen.

"Olaf, leave that thing alone, and let Mrs. Emile have a look."

Anna felt the color rise in her cheeks. The kitchen was warm.

Olaf put out his hand for Anna to shake. His palm was dry and rough. He held Anna's hand hard, almost painfully, crushing the band she wore on her right hand, designed from seven connected ovals, each inscribed with the symbols of the Greek Islands. The ring had been a gift from a man who'd once been interested in her but eventually found her intellect too challenging, though the way he put it was that Anna thought she was "a little above herself."

"Now go on and talk to the neighbors. Your father can't do that all on his own," Britta said.

Olaf released Anna's hand. When he passed by her, she detected a clear scent of lavender soap. Anna turned her attention to the turkey. It had at least another hour to roast. She put it back in the oven, using two spotless white dishtowels to grab the handles of the pan.

"What else are you serving?" Anna asked.

Britta directed her to a bowl of puréed spinach. There was a platter of dried fruit: apricots and figs. Those were expensive, Anna knew. Britta had baked two pies and a cake for dessert. She had put out a plate of crackers and a very bland-tasting cheese which her guests had ignored, she said.

"Olaf can't tolerate the smell of strong cheese in the house," she explained.

"I see."

Probably reminded him of rotting flesh, Anna thought.

"Do you think the turkey will turn out all right?" Britta asked.

"Oh, yes. There won't be a problem."

Britta drew in closer and said that she was overly

nervous because Olaf had a particularly bad day. One of the battles he'd been in had taken place on Christmas Eve, and the memories were pulling him down hard.

"Of course. I understand," Anna said.

She could see Olaf standing in the dining room alone with a glass of something in his hand. He caught Anna's eye. Then he was in the kitchen.

"Would you care for a glass of sherry?" he asked her. "We had it before the Volstead Act, don't worry."

"That would be lovely."

"For you, Mother?"

Britta looked stunned.

"Thank you, son. Yes, I would."

When he'd gone, Britta said, "I never saw him be so chivalrous with anyone. I think he's taken a little fancy to you." Britta giggled. "Let him down gently, won't you?"

"Of course."

That might be hard, Anna thought. She thought Olaf was the most handsome man she'd ever seen. The way he looked at her made her feel like a gorgeous creature.

*

Which is what he took to calling her when he slipped over to her house. His mother had to be out or upstairs napping for him to come. Otherwise, she might ask where he was going and why; he was that closely watched.

Anna served him coffee and biscuits, and listened to him talk. He didn't ramble. His thinking followed clear lines. While the war had changed everything for him, he wasn't ready to give up on life. He was tired of despair. He had decided that even before meeting Anna. She tried to discourage his affection for her, without success. He was clearly smitten, and said so.

"Maybe because it's, you know," he said.

"What?"

"That you're a Jew. I never met one before."

Anna stirred her coffee slowly with a small silver spoon—one of a set she had brought over with her.

"Drawn to the exotic then, are you?" she asked.

"If the exotic looks like you."

He lifted her free hand and kissed it.

"You mustn't do that. I'm a married woman."

Olaf's eyes grew dark.

"I've seen him, you know. Your husband," he said.

"And?"

117

"And nothing. I don't know what all the big talk is about."

"He's a hard worker."

"Do you love him?"

Anna went on stirring her coffee.

"Do you?"

"You are guilty of impertinence."

*

Paul's mood was splendid. He'd received his first evaluation from Professor Plake, and couldn't be more pleased.

"I think come fall, you'll be married to an associate professor," Paul said. Anna watched him spoon out more of her lamb stew onto his plate. He sipped his cider. She noticed a small stain on his shirtfront. She didn't mention it.

Anna pushed the food around on her plate. She set her fork down. She reflected on the New Year's resolution she'd made.

Be steadfast.

Paul watched her.

"You've got quite a glow to you this evening, Anna," he said.

"Have I?"

118

"Are you in the family way?"

Anna's heart beat loudly in her ears, like the tide of an angry sea.

"I shouldn't think so," she said.

"Oh."

She watched his mood darken.

"Are you sure you're really trying?" he asked.

"Trying?"

"You know."

"Yes, Paul, I'm trying."

*

Another time, Olaf talked about the war. He'd killed men, that was to be expected, that's what one was trained to do. He described stabbing men through the stomach with his bayonet. He'd witnessed terrible deaths and terrible injuries. Amputations done right there, in the trenches, out of necessity. He wouldn't have minded losing a limb, he said. Not as bad as being left blind. He'd known many who lost their sight to explosions and shrapnel. It always struck him as odd that those men—all the men—needed their blindness before the war, not after.

They were in Olaf's kitchen that time. Britta and Lars were away for the day. They'd taken the train to Sioux City to meet with a different hardware wholesaler. Better saw blades, Britta said. Cheaper nails, too.

"Sometimes marriage is like war," Anna said.

"Because of the fighting?"

"No, of course not."

She stared into her empty cup.

"Marriage can cause a sort of blindness," she said.

Olaf drank his coffee. He looked amused.

"I'd suggest that being married might alter one's vision," he said.

"What do you mean?"

Again, he looked amused, highly pleased with himself, in fact.

"I mean that he doesn't see you well enough, and that you see him too clearly."

That Olaf had learned her secret without her telling it outright made her adore him even more.

*

No note was left as to where they'd gone, nor why, but the town knew soon enough. Olaf cabled his folks and said not to worry. They were in Chicago, where he planned to go into the restaurant business. He'd told Anna in confidence that he'd made a little money on the black market during the war. It would see them through until they made money of their own. The restaurant would serve Greek and Armenian food, something Anna was naturally well-versed in. Olaf had been shocked to learn that she was an Armenian, for they were a Christian people. Anna told him the truth. She hoped he wasn't disappointed. He wasn't. He didn't care what God, if any, she prayed to.

She took little away with her. Her jewelry, of course, and the prized alabaster box. A mixing bowl she particularly liked, decorated with blue stripes. A book into which she'd pressed flowers years before in Constantinople for luck.

She left her wedding band, which she'd known all along had belonged to Paul's aunt, on the base of the menorah.

trial by luck

The genie didn't look like a genie at all. More like one of those super nerdy guys in high school with glasses and bad skin, Laurie thought. To Jonathon, the genie was a bronzed surfer with flip-flops and a leather band around his neck.

The genie escaped from the spare tire compartment of Jonathon's Toyota. There'd been something in the road, a board, probably, that Laurie saw and Jonathon didn't. She yelled at him to avoid it, and he hit it instead. Laurie had called him an asshole, which made his thick lower lip turn down. They were on a highway outside of Elkhart, Indiana, going to see Laurie's parents, a visit neither wanted to make but felt obliged to since they'd agreed to spring for the lavish wedding Laurie said she wanted.

The genie rose up not in a purple haze or flash of green, but something resembling the dust devils Laurie and Jonathon had seen coursing the deserts of Arizona. In fact, Jonathon remembered thinking at the time how genie-like those dust devils were. He was pleased that he'd correctly guessed the true nature of genies. Laurie, on the other hand, wasn't pleased, with him, the genie, or anything else. She sat on the shoulder of the highway, using her jacket as a cushion. She'd refused to lend a hand when asked, and wondered if it was her refusal that had caused the genie to come to the rescue.

"Here, let me get that for you," the genie said, and *ZAP*, the tire was changed. The couple assumed that their first wish had been granted and that two more would be forthcoming. The genie disabused them.

"This is a one-wish deal, friends," he said.

"You mean, that's it?" Laurie asked. She tended to whine when tense, but always hated the sound it made.

"Not at all. The tire change is gratis. Free. On the house."

"Oh," Jonathon said.

"So, take your time, talk it over, and settle on one wish," the genie said.

"One, for the both of us?" Laurie asked. The whine was still there.

"Yup." Then the genie took himself off in another dust devil.

With him gone, the rushing traffic became noisy again. They wondered if something had happened to their hearing while in the genie's presence. Laurie stood up and brushed herself off. She was hungry and dispirited, which made no sense, she knew. Not with the possibility of being granted a fabulous wish.

"We should get going," she said.

"You don't have to shout."

"I'm not."

"Yes, you are."

They got in the car. The engine took a moment to turn over. Jonathon wished he'd replaced the battery cable as the mechanic had recommended. The car was eight years old and had a lot of miles on it. Maybe they should ask for a new car. When he told Laurie that, she said she couldn't believe what an idiot he was.

"Okay, then. What do you wish for?" he asked. He pulled into traffic and accelerated rapidly. Laurie hated how he drove, hating that she hated that.

"For you to slow down," she said.

"Very funny."

"A good lunch."

"You can have that without the genie's help."

Signs for a family-owned diner appeared up ahead. Jonathon pulled off and followed the directions the sign had given. In a few minutes, they were seated, staring at large, laminated menus, surrounded by the irresistible smell of grilling meat.

Laurie stirred her iced tea. She would have preferred a glass of wine. Jonathon said she loved it too much, and raised an eyebrow when she ordered a second glass in a restaurant. It wasn't even noon, which meant she'd get a snide comment if she asked for some now. Laurie was a marketing executive for the regional cable company. Part of her job was to take potential advertisers out for lunch and dinner. If they ordered an alcoholic beverage, which they almost always did, she looked like a stuck-up prude if she didn't go along. Jonathon was a grant writer for a non-profit organization that protected the rights of illegal immigrants, of which Arizona had a great many. He was dedicated to his work, though he wished he could have put his law degree to better use. He'd been turned down by one law firm after another in Phoenix. He didn't like thinking that he'd settled, but in truth, he had. His sense of failure made him intolerant of personal foibles, Laurie thought. He was judgmental.

"Did it really happen?" she asked him.

"The genie?"

"What else?"

"Looked real to me. But what a surfer dude is doing in the middle of Indiana beats the hell out of me," Jonathon said.

"What are you talking about? The guy's more like a computer geek."

That would be just like Laurie to conceal her attraction to someone by putting him down,

Johnathon thought. Once, when she returned home from an office party, Laurie had complained about one of her co-workers, saying he dressed badly, chewed with his mouth open, and didn't know the difference between Merlot and Cabernet. Later, Jonathon happened to meet the man when he came to pick Laurie up. He was stunningly handsome, tall and blond. The way Laurie looked after him when he went down the hall made Jonathon's stomach lurch.

They ordered lunch.

"I wish it would come soon. I'm starving," Laurie said.

Through the plate glass window, the cars moved in dream-like silence along the freeway. Watching them only agitated Laurie further. She worried about how long the trip was taking. They were already overdue at her parents' house. Her cell phone was dead, or she'd have called them.

Jonathon saw where she was looking, and looked, too.

"Know what my mother used to say? 'All those people going by, and I don't know any of them,'" he said.

"Why are you bringing up your mother?"

"Oh, never mind."

Laurie and Jonathon's mother didn't get along.

126

Jonathon's mother thought Laurie was pushy. Laurie thought Jonathon's mother was narrow-minded. Jonathon was tired of being caught in the middle.

He wrote something on his paper napkin. Laurie watched the tiny bald spot on the top of his head as he leaned forward.

"What are you doing?" she asked.

"Making a list of wishes."

"What do you have so far?"

"Well, money. That's the first thing that comes to mind, right? Lots of money. That we'd split. After that, perfect health until the age of ninety."

"Why ninety?"

"Okay, then, until whenever you want."

"Why not eternal life?"

"Be serious, will you?"

Laurie pushed away her glass of tea. She signaled the waitress, who took a few minutes to swing by. Laurie asked for her wine. Jonathon didn't say anything. He was adding items to his list and studying it.

"I wonder if we could have just one long sentence," he said.

"What?"

"You know. 'We want a trillion dollars and health and three children, also rich and healthy, etc.'"

"Children?"

Jonathon grew annoyed.

"Stop asking stupid questions and focus!" he said.

"Since when is the question of children stupid?"

Laurie's wine arrived. There was no sign of their food.

"Or, how about this? 'We wish for an endless supply of future wishes to be granted,'" he said.

"That's clever; I have to admit."

Jonathon grinned. Laurie wondered if he'd brushed his teeth that morning. Their departure from the motel had been a bit rushed. They'd overslept again. She didn't know why they were both so tired, or deaf to clock-radio alarms. At home, their dog, Pixie, got them up. Jonathon wanted Pixie to come with them, and Laurie said she'd be better off boarding at the place she went during the week for doggie day care. Pixie had trouble being alone in the house when they were at work. She had destroyed all their area rugs and had begun whittling down the dining room table—an expensive Mexican antique.

"I don't think he'll go for that, though. I know I wouldn't, in his shoes," Jonathon said.

"High-topped sneakers, no less."

"What are you talking about? Didn't you see his

flip-flops?"

Laurie again turned to watch the endless flow of vehicles along the freeway. The silence out there was eerie.

She drank her wine, hoping it would take the edge off.

Their food arrived.

"This isn't what I ordered," Laurie said.

"Cheeseburger, toppings on the side, fruit instead of fries," the waitress said. Her glasses were green and perfectly round.

"French dip," Laurie said.

"You sure?"

"Positive."

Jonathon had ordered an omelet which he didn't want.

"Trade with me. I'll eat your burger," he said.

"Oh, all right."

They switched plates.

"Anything else I can get for you folks?" the waitress asked.

"Another glass of wine," Laurie said.

Jonathon cocked his eyebrow. "I didn't realize you'd even had one."

"That's because you weren't paying attention."

The waitress left them alone.

"I'm trying to figure out this wish thing," Jonathon said. He picked up a strawberry from his plate, and put it back down. Laurie poked at her omelet. She wasn't hungry anymore.

"I should find a phone," she said.

"What for?"

"To tell my parents we're running late."

"What happened to your cell?"

"Out of juice."

"Take mine."

He handed her his phone. The background was a picture of her holding Pixie. Pixie was smiling. Laurie wasn't.

"Why didn't you tell me your phone was working?" she asked, trying to figure out how to unlock the screen. She hated his phone. It was too complicated.

"You didn't ask."

She managed to unlock the phone, and punched in the numbers. Nothing happened. She looked at the phone.

"It says I'm not getting a signal," she said.

"Then you're probably not."

"We're on a highway! How can there be no signal?"

"How should I know?"

She pushed her plate away.

"I really wanted that French dip," she said.

"I'll call her back."

"Don't, it's okay."

Jonathon ate his burger. His appetite never failed, no matter what. They could be having the worst fight of their lives, and he'd sit down and plow through a triple-decker sandwich. He managed to stay thin, though. She appreciated that, at least.

He dabbed his lips with his napkin, then put the napkin on his dirty, empty plate.

"You know, I'm having second thoughts about this," he said.

"The wish?"

"Yeah."

"Why?"

"Because no matter what we choose, there will probably come a day when we wish we'd chosen something else."

"I've lived with regrets before."

His eyebrows drew together.

"Like what?" he asked.

"Oh, nothing."

"No, tell me."

131

"You know. Stuff."

"That's not very specific."

"Well, I'm sorry. I can't think of anything off the top of my head."

"Do you regret your career?" he asked.

"No."

"This trip?"

"No!"

"Me?"

"Don't be ridiculous."

He leaned back against the fake red leather vinyl of the booth they sat in.

"That's it, isn't it? You regret saying you'll marry me," he said. His voice was quiet.

"That isn't true!"

Jonathon looked at his watch. He tapped it. He removed it from his wrist and brought it to his ear. He set the watch on the table. He looked around for the waitress. He took out his wallet and put two twenty dollar bills on the table.

"What are you doing? Nothing we ordered cost that much," Laurie said.

He exchanged one of the twenties for a ten.

"Is that better?" he asked. She didn't answer.

He stood up.

"Let's get out of here," he said.

Laurie chugged down the rest of her wine. Just outside the doorway of the diner, Jonathon stopped. He turned and faced her.

"Have you ever noticed that we never see things the same way?" he asked.

"What's that supposed to mean?"

"You know perfectly well what it means. You see things your way, I see things my way, and they're never the same."

"Jesus! What the hell are you talking about?"

He simply stared at her. He seemed shorter than she remembered, which made no sense. Laurie felt fuzzy in the head. She wished she hadn't drunk her wine so fast.

"I need to sit down," she said.

"We're almost at the car."

He took her arm a little roughly and steered her down the sidewalk. The genie was in the driver's seat, fiddling with the radio. He got out.

"All right then, folks, what's the verdict?" he asked.

The whole thing had been a trial, Laurie realized, and they were their own jury. She wondered if the same thought had occurred to Jonathon, given his legal background. But no, it was clear that he was thinking up what to wish for. He had that puzzled look he sometimes got when she said something that went over his head.

She put her face in her hands. "I wish this whole day had never happened," she whispered.

Returned seamlessly to the day before, and now at the wheel, Laurie told Jonathon she wanted to do all the driving from then on out. They were in Nebraska, and the road was a flat black ribbon in the sun.

"Really, why?" he asked.

"I need to stare at the highway for a while. It clears the mind."

"Fine with me."

A tumbleweed bounced across the highway and lodged in the barbed wire fence that followed it for miles. They each thought it looked like a living being, a creature with will and purpose, but neither said so. Jonathon closed his eyes and tried to sleep. Laurie kept driving toward the future, whatever it was.

along came a spider

She was drawn to his watercolors. Gentle landscapes, ponds and rushes, and a sky so soft and blue she wanted to rise and just drift away. His work often had that effect on her. Later pieces, which featured animals and people, all with some sort of minor flaw—an odd skin tone, disproportionate limbs on a dog or horse, a woman's jagged hair made of harsh, black dots—could bring tears to her eyes. He wasn't particularly gifted; they both knew that. But he had passion. That's what counted.

Nonny wrote poems no one wanted to publish, so one day, in a state of exalted frustration, she published them herself online in a blog she named *I Give You My Word*. She didn't know how to promote the blog, however, so the poems went as unnoticed as they had before. Giles thought her poems were fine, well-crafted, especially one which began with the line, "A beam bears or makes light." He didn't know anything about poetry, though. He admitted as much one night after too much to drink in the bar at The Duckbill Inn, where they'd first met and visited when they wanted a taste of nostalgia.

Nonny wasn't young. And she wasn't rich, had no children and had never been married, but she was comfortable. Her father left her some money, which she invested with great care. These facts she attributed to being completely ordinary looking. She was forty-five, medium height, just a little overweight, brown hair that shined only when she had just washed it. Otherwise, it reminded her of a mouse's fur, though mice, Giles informed her, were, in his experience, usually gray.

"Give it time," she replied.

She was pleased with her wit. She was pleased by the quiet atmosphere in the bar that evening, several months into their relationship. She was pleased with Giles, who had about him an air of unrelenting sorrow. She had always been drawn to moody men, perhaps because they reminded her so much of her father, an artist at heart who gave up a love of music to practice law—tax law, the dullest and probably most lucrative kind. What he learned from his clients, he passed on to Nonny, his only child. *Always play the market long, never short. Balance your equities with bonds. Pay attention to emerging markets.* Most of this went over her head, but she knew a winner when she saw one, and so far, she'd been lucky.

They agreed not to marry. Neither saw the point. He moved in with her, though they'd considered having her move in with him. His home was deplorable. That was the only word for the cracked tile floors and strange smudges on the walls, as if in moments of sudden grief he brushed his hands over the uneven surface. The result of a "plastered plasterer," Giles said.

Giles was a tall man with a bad back, which made painting on his feet difficult, so he sat in a wicker chair that wobbled. In Nonny's small, charming cottage, with a full view of the lake from one window and a deep, dense wood from another, the chair and his easel had pride of place in the center of the living room. Nonny once had her writing desk in that same spot, and she gave it up the moment Giles claimed it. She was happy to, and if not happy, at least unperturbed. Giles was like a large planet she became content to orbit around, though her orbit was hardly smooth or regular. He made demands which taxed her, and which he thought should be very easy to accommodate. One of these was his taste for sauerkraut, the smell of which Nonny found nauseating. Giles made his own brine.

Nonny kept churning out her poems, and Giles kept painting. He had a friend in the village who ran a little gallery where his work was sometimes exhibited. The village was a tourist trap, a scenic place fifty miles or so outside the city where day trippers came to eat, drink, marvel, and often part with their plentiful cash. Nonny took a dim view of city people. Giles rather liked them. He particularly liked one older couple who took a fancy to his rendition of a cow, a barn, and a tree that had been struck by lightning. Nonny didn't feel it was his best work and was stunned—even a bit jealous—to learn that the couple bought it for the requested price of five hundred dollars. The couple asked Giles and Nonny to join them for drinks at The Duckbill Inn. Nonny was reluctant to go, yet she didn't want another lecture from Giles about her chronic lack of support. She supported him plenty, particularly in the matter of money, since he seemed to have none of his own.

Nonny made the effort. She put dark shadow on her eyelids and rouge on her cheeks. She clipped back her hair, which gave her a severe appearance. She wanted to look in control, slightly cynical, as if the whole world were there purely for her own amusement. Giles also took pains with his appearance. He shaved and cut himself. The bleeding took time to stop. He fussed with a speck of Kleenex he pressed to the wound. Nonny said he'd be fine and that he should continue to get dressed. He didn't want to bleed on his new shirt.

Nonny didn't know he had a new shirt. He explained that it was a shirt he'd owned for some time, though never had worn. When he put it on, Nonny saw why. It was loud, with wide black and white stripes. But when paired with a pair of black jeans, he looked rather dashing, she had to admit. Better than she did in her wool skirt that was too short, thus revealing too much of her thick thighs, which she tried to hide inside a pair of wool tights. Since the bar at The Duckbill Inn was so warm—an angry fire blazed in the two-hundred-year-old brick fireplace—Nonny found herself sweating almost at once.

The couple, Mr. and Mrs. Baxter, arrived late. Giles had already had one glass of wine and fretted they might not come at all, which would mean he'd have to pay the bill himself. His mood turned sunny the instant they walked into the room.

Mrs. Baxter was old money. Nonny could see that right off. Her silk blouse and wool slacks were stylish though unpretentious. Her hair was short, iron gray, and nondescript. It was her jewelry that said what she was used to. All diamonds—nothing oversized, vulgar, or gaudy, just simply first-rate pieces that Nonny despised herself for admiring. Mr. Baxter looked like a man who spent a lot of time outdoors, probably on a golf course, which, given that he was obviously in his fifties or even sixties, meant he was retired. He had a bit more flash than his wife did. He wore on his pinky a ring with a thick gold band and a fine ruby stone, which Nonny also admired.

They ordered martinis. Nonny continued to nurse her white wine, which she didn't care for. Giles had a second, then a third glass of cabernet. His mood was splendid. He'd always been an artist, he told the Baxters. The Baxters were thrilled. Giles was clearly the real deal. The conversation grew livelier as time passed, though Nonny contributed nothing. A dull ache had settled under her rib after Giles introduced her as "my friend," which earned her a brief appraisal by Mrs. Baxter, a smile from Mr. Baxter, and not a single question about her from either.

She excused herself and escaped to the ladies' room, where she gave herself a long assessment in the floor-length mirror. She decided she was pretty, a conclusion she came to from time to time in moments of growing unease.

When she returned to the table, the Baxters proposed that she and Giles collaborate on producing a children's book. Giles had just told them that Nonny was a writer, and since Giles was such a fine artist, the outcome of their efforts would be brilliant. Nonny took a moment to consider if they were joking. They seemed earnest. She was pretty sure that Giles thought they were a couple of idiots, because how could he not? A book was a serious undertaking, or so she always assumed. Giles immediately accepted their suggestion and turned at once to the question of royalties. It seemed as though the Baxters wanted to bring out the book themselves, under their own imprint. They knew nothing about publishing but would learn, eagerly. Giles would receive fifty percent of any royalties received.

"Which means twenty-five percent for me," Nonny said.

Giles stared at her with bloodshot eyes. He seemed not to understand what she'd just said.

"Do the math," Nonny added.

Mrs. Baxter suggested that they order something to eat. She was flushed with gin. Mr. Baxter looked like he'd overshot his mark, too. Nonny felt like the only adult at a table full of sloppy children. Giles said that since they lived just a hop, skip, and a jump away (his exact words), they should all repair to their house rather than continue occupying the bar.

"I'm afraid our cupboard is bare," Nonny said.

"Nonsense! I just went to the store. And we've got all that fresh fish, remember?" Giles asked.

The fish came from a neighbor who took his boat out whenever he felt a bender coming on. Being loaded on dry land seemed like a more serious affair than having a few on the high seas, he said with surprising candor, so when the urge hit, he made for the water. On that particular day, he offered to take Giles, and Nonny said it was fine if he went, but she would be the last one to notify the Coast Guard when they failed to return on time. The neighbor made the trip alone—and relatively sober, an unexpected benefit of getting a call, out of the blue, from his ex-wife to say she missed him. He came back with a freezer full of cod that he was kind enough to gut himself before passing about three pounds' worth to Nonny and Giles.

"Oh, I'm not really a fish person," Mrs. Baxter said. She looked at her watch.

Mr. Baxter was staring at Nonny. Nonny looked away.

"We need to devise the plot," Mr. Baxter said.

"What plot?" Giles asked. He'd been looking around for the waiter, who had disappeared.

"Of your wonderful book, of course!" Mr. Baxter boomed.

"Our wonderful book, you mean," Mrs. Baxter said.

"Plot?" Giles asked again.

"As in the beginning, the middle, and the end," Nonny said. Her mood was improving. She intended to give Giles a piece of her mind once they were alone.

"A remake of Little Miss Muffet," Mr. Baxter suggested.

"But, Horace. That's just a nursery rhyme,"

Mrs. Baxter said.

"That was Claire's favorite. Don't you remember?" Mr. and Mrs. Baxter grew quiet. Their silence continued.

Nonny moved her glass of wine a few inches along the smooth surface of the red linen tablecloth.

"You want us to produce a children's book based on a nursery rhyme? Is that it?" she asked. Like a gust of wind on a day that had otherwise been completely still, the idea suddenly took shape in her mind. A new portrayal of the spider as the victim of Miss Muffet's ignorance, a general exposé of the importance of insects and their place in the animal kingdom, maybe borrowing a little from *Charlotte's Web*: the idea of a spider as a savior and Little Miss Muffet as an ignorant, uptight imbecile. But then people who thought that little girls should be encouraged to achieve and be confident would object to that characterization, however subtly presented. Little Miss Muffet would have to be a heroine in her own right, too. The spider and Miss Muffet could join forces and take on the world's problems—the spider with her ability to spin the truth out of filaments of fact, and Miss Muffet the spokesperson for any number of worthy, humane causes.

"You look like you've had too much to drink," Giles said to Nonny. He made sure to put a little tease in his voice so it wouldn't sound like the rebuke it really was. Not a rebuke against her consumption of alcohol, of course, because she'd had only the one glass of wine. His displeasure came from what he read as a look of pure joy.

*

Though Nonny never spoke of her, she was often on her mind. The woman her father took up with after her mother walked out. Her name was Arabelle. Arabelle had a habit of getting fixated on something, a flaw usually, a smudge on the ceiling or a crack in a cabinet door, which caused her to stop what she was doing and consider. What was there to consider? Nonny never understood. Either you sought to solve a problem, or you didn't. Simple problems didn't get any clearer just because you pondered them longer. It wasn't what her eyes fell on that obsessed Arabelle, however, but what they represented in her own life. The hold Nonny's father kept on his money, to be exact. His reluctance to spend on niceties, pleasures of any kind. Not a Scrooge exactly, because he was decent to Nonny and allowed her the things she both needed and wanted. Her tastes were plain. He never had to dip too far into his accounts to accommodate her, except once.

Nonny had just gotten her driver's license. She

was careful, even hyper vigilant, behind the wheel. She never had tasted alcohol or smoked pot. Her life was quiet and proper. On that particular day, Nonny's father let her drive herself to school. He owned two cars: a Lincoln Continental and a twenty-year-old Mercedes Benz. The Mercedes was a stick shift, so Nonny drove the Lincoln. Arabelle was put out, because she thought of the Lincoln as her personal car to use whenever she wanted, though she seldom went anywhere except into town to look at clothes, add up prices, then prepare another campaign to persuade Nonny's father why she should have them. Arabelle had a little money of her own from a previous marriage but felt it was beneath her to spend it.

Nonny was asked to stay after school to go over an English paper she'd written—her very first attempt at poetry. *If you want me to, I will / If you force me to, I won't / for this is the law of a woman's heart / which beats for herself alone.*

The teacher didn't comment on her literary brilliance but asked about the origin of that particular passage. Nonny was at a loss. Her teacher, Mr. Neville, was in his late forties, which made him ancient in Nonny's eyes. He was short and round, the kind of person who should have a jolly, cheerful air, but not Mr. Neville. His shoulders slumped, and his voice was tinged with sadness, as if everything he said might, at any moment, touch upon some great tragedy.

"I won't mince words," Mr. Neville said. "We are here to protect our precious students. I want to know if you have met with harm. If someone has harmed you or threatened to."

"Me? No! Of course not!" Nonny couldn't imagine that there was anything in her demeanor that would give that impression. She was pink-cheeked and energetic, if on the quiet side. She typically kept to herself, but she did have one or two good friends, other serious girls like herself with whom she would sometimes giggle in class. She had to think, as Mr. Neville looked her in the eye, that his concern stemmed from knowing about her mother's abandonment. Her father had gone to the school to make everyone aware of the situation. He didn't ask the staff to do anything in particular, just to be alert to signs of unhappiness that he might overlook.

"You're sure?" Mr. Neville asked. He sounded exhausted.

"Yes."

"Well, then. You have the makings of a fine poet."

It was getting dark on her way home. Dead leaves rushed across the pavement. Drops of rain fell onto the windshield. Nonny turned on her lights. She kept her eye on the speedometer. The impact was so slight she didn't register it at first. Not until she was at the stop sign thirty feet beyond did she become aware of someone shouting, another person running, and the rain coming down much harder.

The little girl was only eight. She wasn't wearing a helmet. Her bicycle was new, with plastic tassels hanging from each handlebar. At first the blow to her head didn't seem too bad, then her condition worsened, and by the time a neurosurgeon had been flown in from Providence, she was gone.

One witness said she'd veered into Nonny's car. Another corroborated that. The question was, why hadn't Nonny seen her? She considered this at the police station with her father at her side.

"Something caught my eye," Nonny said. She was pretty sure she was going to wake up any minute and wonder what was for breakfast.

"What was it?" The investigator wore a tweed jacket, nothing like a regular police officer. That, and his patient voice—so like Mr. Neville's earlier in the afternoon, though really, it wasn't possible that all of this was happening on the same day—told Nonny to take her time and answer carefully.

"Something small and dark. It was there, then not there," Nonny said. It was all she could recall.

Later, in a private meeting with Judge Richards, a friend of Nonny's father, it was stated that Nonny had no history of mental disorders. She was not given to hallucinations. The meeting was held at the request of Nonny's father. Though Nonny hadn't been formally charged in the matter of the little girl's death, her name should be cleared, once and for all. And it was, the minute the district attorney declined to prosecute.

But the child's parents couldn't be kept still. They wanted to bring a civil suit of wrongful death. Nonny's father met with them and their lawyer and made it clear, as their lawyer already knew, that they'd never win a dime. The child had just learned to ride the bicycle. She'd gone out, alone, at rush hour. She was clearly unsupervised, and though it pained him to say it, the parents were just looking for someone to blame for their own negligence.

Yet a few weeks later, the family received an envelope containing a large sum of cash. When Nonny's father was asked by a reporter if he'd been the benefactor, he calmly denied any involvement whatsoever.

"Just some good soul, feeling their grief, who wanted to be of help," he said. Nothing more was ever said on the matter.

Nonny never determined what the small, dark

thing was that caught her attention for that split second. In time, she thought it was any number of things—a leaf, a bird, an evil spirit. It was Arabelle who suggested it was a spider, which Nonny found apt. Arabelle with her plans and schemes knew all about spiders, didn't she? Over the years, Arabelle came and went as her patience—or lack thereof—with Nonny's father's grip on his assets got the better of her. One day she went away for the last time, and Nonny was both saddened and shocked to discover her father weeping silently in his study.

*

Nonny's idea was that Little Miss Muffet and the spider should become fast friends and travel the world. Little Miss Muffet would provide a portable web for the spider, conveniently named Arabelle. The web would be housed in a porous piece of cloth around Miss Muffet's neck. The web, on a fancy wooden stand, would sit in the windowsill of whatever grand hotel room they occupied so that Arabelle could catch flies. When they returned home, the spider would chronicle their adventures in arachnese, the language of web weavers, which Little Miss Muffet would preserve for all time.

"It's retarded," Giles said.

"It has a message."

Giles snorted. He was drinking. His mood was bad. He'd had a postcard from his ex-wife asking for money. Apparently they came every couple of years. This one claimed the usual urgency. He read it to her: *Darling. This time I'm serious. PLEASE!*

"Darling?" Nonny asked.

"She's sort of melodramatic."

The card was from Athens. Nonny didn't see how someone who had gotten herself to Greece in the first place needed money. Giles explained that the last he'd heard, the ex-wife was working in a hotel over there. Maybe the job ended or she'd gotten fired and couldn't find new work. Didn't she know by now that Giles had nothing to give her? Then the other shoe fell. He did have something to give her—the money from the trust account he managed on her behalf.

Nonny went into her modest kitchen with its plastic countertops and old appliances and poured herself a glass of the nice French wine Giles had bought the other day to celebrate the Baxters' patronage. The kitchen had a built-in banquette in the corner by a window that looked into the back garden. A deer stood there, nibbling the rose blossoms just opening on the only surviving bush. Four of the original five that Nonny had planted, in an uncharacteristic fit of zeal, had died. They stood nearby, a chorus of thorny, brown stalks. Nonny had lacked the energy to remove them.

Giles joined her.

"I didn't tell you because it's not my money," Giles said.

"Why are you in charge of it?"

He sat, crowding her on the banquette. It was a complicated story, he said. His wife, Meredith, had a history of mental illness. She had mood swings and was given to bouts of frantic anxiety. She was very young when they met, only eighteen. He felt protective of her. He couldn't help it. He supposed that was why he married her in the first place. She was attractive enough, but he wanted—he didn't really know—to make her *better.*

Nonny had trouble seeing this trait in Giles. He was hardly protective of her, nor nurturing for that matter. She had begun to wonder lately if she had made a mistake. She wasn't sure she was happy with him. Just the night before, she told herself to hang on long enough to complete the Baxters' project. Listening to him then, she was moved by his candor and the dark light in his eyes as he recalled it all, as if the world around him had just melted away and he was back in time, giving his heart to this wretched, afflicted woman.

Life with Meredith was no picnic, Giles said. The constant ups and downs. The creeping fear that she might do away with herself. She mentioned suicide more than once. Her family was glad then that Giles was in her life. It became his full-time job to keep an eye on her. Always a little uneven in the employment department, Giles willingly gave up working at a paint store to stay home with Meredith. While he hated advising wannabe artists on how to mix and blend colors, he found that he preferred it to endlessly trying to keep Meredith amused. Things between them quickly soured. Meredith was, by turns, manic, full of unstoppable energy— running him ragged with her schemes to redecorate the small apartment her parents paid for, a new hobby she took up like yoga or belly dancing—then she always collapsed, stayed in bed, refused to speak. Doctors were no help. Medication did nothing. Giles lost patience. They quarreled. They accused each other of not caring.

Then came the physical part. The pushing and shoving. Meredith would get frustrated with some tiny thing, blame him, and want to hurt him. He didn't take it seriously at first. She was so small and weak. But then she hit him with an umbrella and left a painful bruise. He threatened to leave her. She went on a verbal assault about each and every one of his faults. He was stupid, talentless, would never amount to anything. She did him a favor by staying, because who else would want him? He was stuck with her; he'd just have to go on taking it because he lived off her parents. He'd better watch his step, too, because she could cancel the arrangement just like that. She even snapped her fingers when she said this. To Nonny it all sounded so childish and clichéd, but she could hear in Giles' voice how important it had been to him then, how important those words of Meredith's still were.

Giles wasn't proud of it, but the fact was, he started drinking. She drove him to it, he said. And when he drank, his temper sometimes got the better of him. He broke things. Bowls, glasses, and a radio all got hurled at the exposed brick wall of their apartment. The neighbors called the police more than once. Giles was even taken to the station once and interviewed in a hostile manner. No one could believe that it was his wife who was the instigator.

One day, when Meredith was pouring it on again, he pushed her down the stairs right outside their door. He couldn't say he hadn't meant to. He didn't recall just what he'd been thinking at the time, only that enough was enough. Meredith landed badly and broke her collarbone. No one witnessed the fall, and later, she swore to the authorities that she'd stumbled. Her blood alcohol level lent truth to the story. Somehow, after all her cruelty toward him, she couldn't bring herself to make a formal accusation. He took it as a token of the love which he knew had been there all along. Yet they couldn't go on living together. They both knew that. They separated, then divorced. Meredith's father was prepared to go on being the administrator of the trust he'd established for her years before, but Meredith insisted that control of her assets be turned over to Giles. The father took a lot of persuading, apparently, though Giles wasn't privy to the exact details of his difficult conversations with Meredith.

Nonny asked why Meredith couldn't handle her own affairs. She was an adult, wasn't she?

Meredith lacked the confidence to pay attention to money. She was afraid that if she had complete access to it, she'd run through it in no time. Her parents were dead. She didn't want to turn to other family members, with whom she'd never been very close. Giles was the only one she could trust. And he had to do it, because Meredith had kept his secret.

"But who would care now, after all this time, if she told the truth? You could always deny it. You weren't named in any report," Nonny said.

"You don't understand."

That was true. She didn't.

*

Nonny gave up on the idea of Little Miss Muffet traveling with the spider. Instead, she thought the spider should teach Little Miss Muffet to weave. Little Miss Muffet would become so successful that her tapestries would be known far and wide. Again, Giles expressed only lukewarm interest in this narrative. He was hard at work. He'd given up watercolors for the moment and was using charcoal. His time seemed to be spent on the spider itself. When Nonny suggested that he move on to something else, like a scene or setting, he told her to go write another one of her stupid poems. That stung. She demanded an apology, which he gave, only because he wanted to be left alone with his easel.

Giles was contrite later that day and on into the evening. He said he'd been unfair to her, and he hoped she'd forgive him. He knew he could be a real pain. Hearing from Meredith had unsettled him. Nonny hadn't asked if he'd complied with her request for money. She assumed he had.

That weekend, the Baxters were in town again. Giles invited them over. He wanted to show them his concept for the spider. Nonny was on edge. She was no good at entertaining. Giles told her not to worry. He'd been in touch with the gourmet food store down the road, and a nice plate of hors d'oeuvres was being put together for them. That sounded expensive to Nonny. She tried not to worry. If the book went well—when she finally pulled the story line together—it was going to be a big hit. She was sure of that.

Rather than dressing up as he had the first time around, Giles remained in his work clothes—old jeans and an oversized sweatshirt. He didn't shave. His hands were smeared with black charcoal. It was important to look the part. Nonny didn't change either. All day she'd been in a floor-length black skirt and a green turtleneck sweater that the advancing season made too warm. She added a heavy necklace of silver beads that had belonged to her mother. It had taken her years to find the courage to wear it. She'd worn it the night she met Giles, and she thought now that it had brought her luck, because they were going to be all right, after all. They were going to be better than all right.

Nonny went to get the hors d'oeuvres. She was disappointed to see some deviled eggs. She couldn't stand deviled eggs. The miniature quiches looked okay, and so did the selection of fruit and cheese.

The Baxters were at the cottage when she returned. They were already enjoying the very good French wine Giles had bought that afternoon. Everyone was happy. Giles had his drawings spread out on the table. Nonny put the food on the counter,

156

said hello, and joined the others in their perusal of the pictures. Nonny was excited. She was seeing them for the first time, too. She had made it a point not to glance at Giles' easel while he was working, so that her impression could be fresh. The spider was in a variety of playful poses and settings. In some, she was in her web. In others, she was dangling from a single thread or scurrying across the floor. She had a human face, and always the same face, with round blue eyes, a pert nose, and full red lips. And she had human hair, a trim black bob. What the Baxters admired most was her tender expression. They were completely enchanted.

Nonny poured Mrs. Baxter another glass of wine. Mr. Baxter consumed a deviled egg in one bite. Nonny asked if everyone would like to move to the living room, where they could be more comfortable. Giles had thoughtfully put his easel away so the path to the sitting area was clear. Nonny brought out the tray of food and some cheerful red paper napkins. She lit the two tall candles on the mantelpiece. She put in a DVD of light jazz and wondered if she should open a window since she was feeling so warm at the moment.

Back in the kitchen, alone, she patted cold water on her face. Something flashed in the corner of her eye. When she turned to look, it was gone. Early in their relationship, Nonny had asked Giles about his ex-wife: what she looked like, how she behaved. Giles said it didn't matter. Nonny pressed. The woman he reluctantly described, with a definite frown on his own face, had blue eyes, red lips—because of her obsession with a shade called "fire engine"—and short, black hair. Overall, she gave the impression of being something between a little girl and a grown woman. It gave her a certain charm, especially when she was gentle, at peace with the world.

Even now, after all these years, Nonny thought. She dried her hands on a clean towel hanging in the handle of the refrigerator.

In the living room, Mr. Baxter asked Giles if he and Nonny were going to give the spider a name. Giles said of course they were.

"Any ideas?" Mrs. Baxter asked.

Nonny stole herself out into the welcome darkness of her backyard before she could hear Giles' reply.

by the wayside

She's a woman who discards anything which causes sorrow or blocks her path. A man she cares for does both, and she leaves him. She takes only what she really values, an old set of books, a few china plates of her mother's, an abstract painting she'd found in Santa Fe, New Mexico. She abhors clutter, both physical and spiritual. She has friends with children, husbands, and houses full of junk, plastic bins, cardboard boxes, old newspapers in piles on the porch, unraked leaves on the walk, and all the time they complain about the mess and the chaos, the failure to effect order, the misuse of their time, and though their company is amusing for an evening, she is always glad—relieved—to return to her own modest place that's clean, stripped down to its essentials.

One clear night, she dreams of her brother standing in a field. The field is unknown, but she recognizes the distant tree, with its unique twist and sagging branch. That tree stood across the road from their home until a strong wind sent a severed branch onto a power line. Men came and cut down the rest of the tree. In her dream, the tree returns and the brother comes to celebrate the miracle.

In the morning, she learns that her brother had

died four days before. They hadn't spoken for thirty years. His erratic behavior became a liability. Late-night rambling phone calls, borrowing money and never paying it back, always an undercurrent of resentment that she was functional and self-supporting while he was neither. After she refused his calls, she had random news of him through her parents. Both hinted at mental illness, trouble holding a job, a string of temporary girlfriends. Nothing was ever clearly stated or described. Truth was messy and took up space, and it, too, was winnowed. The parents are both dead now, the father's second wife, who was never a real presence, is also. Only she remains.

A letter arrives from the man her brother had made his life with. *He worked for a long time to put his childhood rage behind him. I believe he died happy, more or less.*

Her return letter contains only two words: *Why rage?*

He felt like he'd been thrown away, the man replies.

In her dismay, she takes on a comforting chore: cleaning out her closet. There's a blouse she hasn't worn in the last year, also a pair of red shoes, and a photo album she doesn't remember bringing from her last residence. On one page, her family stands in a row. They're by a lake in autumn. The trees are shedding their leaves, and she wears a light little sweater with roses around the collar. It's been so long she can't even name the year, or her age, only that she was happy then, and her brother was, too. They were friends, allies in mischief, united against the growing misery of their parents, safe in their own world.

Her tears surprise her, because she is not a woman who cries. Not when her father left to lighten his load; or when her house was sold; or when her childhood memories disappeared in the back of a truck bound for the dump; or when she fled her only marriage after fifteen months; or when each man had served his time and went; or when she moved the first, fifth, or eleventh time; or when her mother died at home alone; or when her father fell down his basement stairs and never regained consciousness.

Only now, when she sees, as she will over and over, that sometimes—in fact more often than not—the heart is made weaker for leaving behind what once gave it joy.

letters of love and hate

She envied the female diarists, scribbling at elegantly carved desks in great houses. Feather pens, dripping ink, and the thin glow of candlelight. By day they oversaw their families and servants, at night they confided to the page. For the most part they recounted their own small lives. Sometimes, though, they dared to broach a broader topic from the world of men. Slavery, perhaps, or insane asylum brutality or the curse of debtors' prison. Even so, their opinions were kept private. Back then, women didn't write letters to the press. Times had changed. Now the world fed on streams of information, data, loudly voiced opinions. Anyone could speak. The trouble was finding someone to listen.

Cammy J for Jane graduated from Vassar College. In her grandmother's day, it was a place to gain the social skills necessary for a successful life. These included how to set a lovely table, make witty conversation, and gently, but firmly, rebuff the inappropriate advances of a young man who'd had too much to drink. Cammy J's mother stomped around the campus in torn blue jeans and demonstrated against the Reagan administration. The Vassar College Cammy J attended continued its tradition of keeping pace with the times. She sat in class with the openly gay and transgender. Also with a surprising number of Arabs, who both fascinated and alarmed her. She was not a xenophobe. However, 9/11 had happened. There was no denying it. Yet these Muslim students didn't seem all that wound up, certainly not about their faith. They seemed grounded in the moment, even a bit bogged down by the normal demands of life, which focused on their cell phones and Twitter accounts. There was no madness in their eyes, just a keen intelligence which she imagined was much like hers.

She called her article "They're Just Like Us."

Its final paragraph read: *Why all the animosity toward these people of goodwill, who come here just to learn and be a part of this wonderful American dream? The feet of many nations have trod upon our shores. We must welcome them with open arms and hearts.*

The first response came from her father. James Pritchett took a dim view of his daughter's journalistic efforts, an even dimmer view of her nascent politics.

"You understand, of course, that you're just putting them down. These are smart, tough people you're writing about here. You make them sound like charity cases," he said.

JP, as he insisted on being called, had done very well as a day trader. He was a numbers man, an

163

analyst. "Stay ahead of the curve," he always told her. "Never believe that life is a law of averages." The article was too important to send in an email he could delete, and came to him by her own hand. She had something to prove, namely that the world wasn't one big betting parlor, that there were things more important than money, or making money. Humanity had a value aside from a dollar sign. JP had heard all of this from her before, naturally. He had trained himself, at the urging of his wife (a stony yet broad-minded person), to hold his tongue. But on the matter of his daughter's prose, it was hard to contain himself. He was uneasy. Sooner or later Cammy J might turn her talent with words against him. He imagined the contempt she would unleash. He was sure she despised him. He was sure that she—and everyone—saw in him the desperate, needy young man he used to be.

Cammy J's brother, Hubert, read her piece and scoffed along the same lines as their father.

"Don't denigrate, dumbass," was his advice. Hubert hadn't joined his father's asset management firm. He wanted to be his own man. He had to compensate for being stuck with the name of some moldy forebear. He turned it to his advantage. He was an "elite concierge." He had a list of wealthy clients, often referred by his father, who came to the

City and wanted to rent a luxury apartment for a few weeks or, on occasion, even buy one. He insisted that he was not a realtor. He didn't self-promote. He didn't hustle. He radiated calm and poise, despite the way he spoke to his sister. It was an old thing between them, that animosity. Or rather, the animosity flowed from him much more than from her. Cammy J had always been their mother's favorite, though if one were to ask Cammy J if that were true, she'd look stunned.

Cammy J's mother, Elaine, reviewed the article with detachment. Since her rowdier college days, and especially after marrying and becoming a mother, she'd viewed most of life that way. She was passionate about only two things: martinis and her beloved rescue Great Danes. A large number of them had passed through their home over the years, often happily destroying some pricey treasure, like a pair of crystal candlesticks, but Elaine remained devoted to their care. When the time came to send them on their way, her other passion occupied her time until the next cast-off could be assimilated.

After college, Cammy J moved down to the city and got an unpaid position with a foundation that helped at-risk youth. She'd been told she'd be assisting a caseworker, since she mentioned during her interview that she might one day attend graduate school and earn a Master's of Social Work, which, she was sure, would complement her degree in Anthropology very well. Rather than help her learn the process of managing clients, the caseworker had her file forms, make sure the coffee pot was full, and remind people in the waiting room not to smoke. Cammy J wrote of her experiences there in terms of wasted resources, a willingness to help that was overlooked, and that in this day and age, when government funding was scant and volunteers were needed more than ever, not taking advantage of her energy and education was a sin.

A sin? Once again, JP had to shake his head. But he grudgingly admired his daughter's growing confidence on the page. She was acquiring sass. He liked a sassy woman, in moderation.

Soon Cammy J realized that no one was interested in publishing her articles, so she started a blog. *Straight from the Heart* she called it. She found a graphic of a heart with an arrow through it. Her friend, Lizzie, called her up to say that the image didn't match the title.

"How so?" Cammy J asked. She was at home, in her spacious apartment on the Upper East Side that she'd tried to decorate in a distinctly bohemian style with mismatched furniture, some of which came from the Goodwill. Her efforts were hampered by the original art on the walls. The annual income from her trust fund was generous.

"You need to say, 'straight *to* the heart.' Obviously, the heart's been shot."

Lizzie lived in a Chelsea loft on the same block with galleries that showed her sculptures of human faces made out of rubber. When Cammy J suggested once that these faces looked like Halloween masks from the local party supply store, Lizzie was crestfallen. She continued her work in the same vein, however. Her resilience was admirable.

"Damn it!" Cammy J said.

"An easy fix."

"I'll have to find another name for the blog!"

"Shouldn't be too hard. You'll see."

Cammy J thought and thought. It came to her late one night when she awoke from a restless sleep. She had witnessed something disturbing that very day, downtown, on her way back from meeting Lizzie for lunch. A man was being arrested. The officers had cuffed him and required that he lie on the sidewalk while they completed their paperwork. A grown man, lying on the sidewalk like a dog! A shackled dog, no less. Would he have been so harshly treated if he'd been white? She couldn't see how. She renamed her blog *The Broken Heart.* She railed against the police department, hinting strongly that they were so used to practicing brutality that they'd lost their sense of shame, not to mention compassion. She'd gathered some Twitter followers over the past few months, drawn from classmates, friends of her parents, and even Hubert's clients, whom she'd followed just so they'd follow her back. She read up on promoting oneself through social media. She sent out the link to her article. She invited everyone to post comments. She received two comments. One was from someone identifying himself as Ronald 123.

You're a dingbat. Actually, you're probably worse, but I'm too nice a guy to say exactly what.

The other was from someone named Flora. She checked her list of followers. No Floras. But this was the magic of Twitter, wasn't it? You tweeted, other people retweeted you. You were—what was the word? Disseminated. Spread through the world like fluffy seeds, ready to land, take root and grow.

Except that Flora's comment wasn't particularly generative.

The guy probably did something rotten. Don't they all?

They? THEY? Cammy J was rattled, totally taken aback. Was it possible that she had lived her whole life in a bubble and not really known, never really seen, what it meant to be an African-American in this country? Then, how could she have? In her hometown of Rye, she didn't know many African-Americans. Who were they, exactly? Marcus, whose father was a famous eye surgeon. He volunteered his time to the poor and underserved just as Cammy J had hoped to do. Where she failed, he succeeded. Then there was Mariah. Mariah's mother was a painter and had a gallery on Madison Avenue. Mariah vacationed in Switzerland. Cammy J wondered what Mariah thought of her own race, what it was like for her to cross paths with blacks who were much worse off. Or anyone, really, who was struggling.

Cammy J put this question to her mother.

"I doubt she thinks about it much, do you?" Cammy J's mother asked over an ice cold appletini served with flourish by a very handsome blond waiter—a real Hitler Youth type, Cammy J thought—at the restaurant they'd chosen for lunch.

Cammy J examined her salad. Some of the greens looked a bit wilted around the edges.

"I wish I knew," Cammy J said.

"Tell me, when you run across a homeless person—white, black, doesn't matter—what goes through your mind?" her mother asked.

Cammy J avoided homeless people. It was the look in their eyes she couldn't bear, not when it was desperate or seeking, but distant, absent, as if the soul within was too far away to be reached with a mere handout.

"I'm not sure what you're getting at," Cammy J said.

Her mother sipped her drink. The brooch on the lapel of her silk suit was in the shape of a peacock. Cammy J loved that brooch, and hoped one day it would be hers.

"Are they real to you, these people?" her mother asked.

"Of course they're real."

They weren't, though. They were just part of the landscape. Poor people, homeless people didn't exist for Cammy J the way everyone else did, somehow. Was it because she felt guilty? Because they scared her? Because she found them disgusting?

"You can always do something for them, you know. We do," Cammy J's mother said. She looked at her lamb chop with complete disinterest and ordered a second drink.

"You donate money."

"To a number of different agencies. I can't name them at the moment. Your father would know."

"You get a big tax deduction for doing it."

"Yes, that's true. But we also like to help."

Help, thought Cammy J. *Help?* Those ladies in their great houses probably had known all about that.

170

Rolling up their silk sleeves in time of war and illness. To get one's hands dirty, that's what help was. Not writing a check in the comfort of your wood-paneled office.

Cammy J shared her thoughts.

"Your father's office isn't wood-paneled," her mother said. Her lamb chop continued to lie untouched. "I had it all redone just last year, don't you remember? He hates that wallpaper I chose, but I think it's rather his style. You know, somber and serious."

Cammy J watched the busboy at the far end of the room. His brown face above his white jacket was a taunt, a gambit for her to up the ante. Why were the waiters never dark-skinned, only the underlings?

"Do you feel all right, dear? You look a bit wan," Cammy J's mother said.

Cammy J nodded. Then she said, "It's not right. We should all be doing more."

"You could work at a shelter or a food bank. It might be just the thing. Though if you do, for God's sake, dress appropriately. You know my friend Helen? She did a stint at a shelter on 53rd street. Had her watch stolen. Took it off to do the dishes, which wasn't even her job, but someone called in sick or something, and when she remembered to look for it, it was gone. A Rolex, too. I told her she was silly to wear it around people like that."

"People like what?"

"Don't be naïve. People who steal something to pawn."

Cammy J didn't typically wear expensive things. She found them vulgar. Except for her Jimmy Choo shoes and matching bag. And her Kate Spade jeans and little T-shirt with that charming pink bow on the back collar. She'd never really given her possessions much thought. Now, they filled her with a remorse so heavy and deep it was like stepping into quicksand.

"How did we get onto this subject? I seem to have lost track," Cammy J's mother said.

"We were talking about whether or not people were real. Or whether they seemed real."

"Hm. Well, I hope the waiter is real. Where is he, anyway? I'd like another of these marvelous appletinis."

By the time Cammy J had steered her mother into a cab, she felt rotten.

That night she poured out her heart to her computer.

We are all, each and every one of us, a failure. To not know, to not even see, the condition of thousands of our fellow citizens is a terrible blindness, and of the worst kind, for it comes from eyes that are focused always on the wrong things, a gaze that hungers for comfort and luxury, rather than the necessary task of leveling the playing field. And if that task, that essential human task, proves too arduous, requiring too long a reach of resources or imagination, then we must aim our sights on raising the fortunes of just one person. This war— and it is truly a war—comes down to the might of one to make right.

She called her blog entry "The Power of One."

There were more responses this time.

You go girl! said Charlie Z.

Been there, done that, got the T-shirt, offered Lucy D.

Get over yourself. This country has poured a shitload of money into raising those slobs up and out of poverty. And before you call me a racist, I'm not talking just about blacks, here. I grew up in rural Kentucky, where the poor are as white as milk. Nothing helps. Nothing. Change must come from within. This was from Zandie.

If you're not part of the solution, you're part of the problem, Cammy J was tempted to reply. But she refused to waste her time engaging with people whose opinions were set.

She unburdened herself to Lizzie. They were in Lizzie's studio, a makeshift area at the end of the loft she lived in. Her father had objected to buying it, saying it had no resale value, which made Lizzie say he should think with his heart, not his bank account.

"You need a project," Lizzie said. "You're bored. Being bored makes you frantic."

"I'm not frantic. I'm just upset."

"Upper-class guilt."

"Is not."

"Is so."

Cammy J poured herself more wine. Lizzie was right. Cammy J was full of guilt. She had guilt to the gills.

Lizzie drew her legs up onto the huge pillow she was nestled on. Lizzie was a tiny person with a fierce expression that made her seem like a little girl a lot of the time. Cammy J wondered if she were aware of this—if she struggled to overcome the perception that she was incompetent.

"What if you could wave a magic wand and in one instant erase all inequality?" Cammy J asked.

"Things wouldn't stay equal for long. Some people would do better, just like they do now."

"Some people will always have more talent, you mean?"

"Not talent. Luck." Lizzie's tone was rueful. She hadn't sold one of her faces for quite a while. Artists she deemed less worthy were cleaning up, or so she thought. She didn't really know; she simply assumed that it was her lot to always be on the bottom. Secretly she believed that her own privileged background made her something of a fraud—that her suffering wasn't real, that her vision wasn't keen and incisive, and that this in turn was why her work wasn't sought. She was the victim of ruthless Karma—she didn't really need the money, so she didn't make any.

"People succeed because the odds are stacked in their favor," Lizzie continued. "They're … connected. It's like there's this network of power brokers. It's not what you know, but who you know. You're either in, or you're not. Poor people are never in. They can't *get* in."

"They get in sometimes. Look at President Obama."

"Yeah, but he's smart. If you're not smart, you're always on the outside."

"Of course he's smart! Dumbshits don't get elected president."

They both though of W. Lizzie's point fizzled. Cammy J sighed. They drank more wine and felt even gloomier.

Within the week, Lizzie had sold not just one, but three of her masks to a Frenchman wanting to decorate his Manhattan pied-á-terre. His enthusiasm for her work was expressed in sweeping gestures with both arms and rocking forward onto the balls of his feet. Lizzie had no idea what he was saying. The year she'd spent in Paris had been occupied with drinking and blowing her father's money on stunning little outfits that she quickly tired of and sold to a consignment shop in the Village. She invited Cammy J to join her for a lovely dinner, on her. Cammy J couldn't bring herself to accept. She was still flooded with malaise. She wished she'd been the daughter of a bus driver or a steel worker. But then her life would be hard, and that would have made her bitter and envious of people like herself—the person she really was.

No point in wishing she were anyone else.

She hated to admit it, but her mother was right. She had time; she must spend it wisely. She presented herself at a homeless shelter for battered women the next morning. She entered through a heavy glass door which opened only after someone inside had pressed a buzzer. She had to speak into an intercom and state her business. The long pause between saying she wanted to volunteer and the sound of the buzzer suggested that she wasn't necessarily being taken seriously.

The hall she walked down was lit with fluorescent lights and smelled strongly of boiled cabbage. Cork boards lined either side with various community service messages about getting tested for HIV and other sexually transmitted diseases; hotline numbers to report abuse and assault; enrolling children in Headstart; qualifying your child for free and reduced lunch in the public schools; drug counseling services; even a free weight-loss program offered through a nearby YMCA. Cammy J felt her spirits lift.

The volunteer office was across from the cafeteria, which meant the cabbage smell was even stronger. Lunch was being set up. Two skinny white women, both with dreadlocks and wearing aprons, were setting out big bowls of something on each of the folding tables lined up in the room. One had a nose ring. Cammy J found it distasteful, and made herself look away and focus on what the woman sitting behind the desk was saying to her.

"You need a criminal background check, but if you're wanting to start today, that's fine. We run the prints through the State, and until they come back, the only thing you can't do is be alone with any of the children. There always has to be another staff person present," the woman said. She had thick glasses and an Hispanic accent. Her face was young. Her manner wasn't.

"I see."

The woman—Andrea, she'd said—looked

closely at Cammy J. Cammy J had tried hard that morning to look the part. Her nail polish was clear. Her blouse and slacks were both Navy blue. She wore comfortable, sensible shoes: Calvin Kline loafers. Her jewelry was modest, a thin gold bangle on her wrist and small diamond studs for earrings.

"What will my duties be?" Cammy J asked.

"Right. Sorry. Well, basically, you help out. Whatever's needed. Get clean linens for a cot. Round up a spare toothbrush and toothpaste. Sort out the donations when they come in, which isn't often."

"Donations?"

"Things people give us. Free stuff." Andrea's tone was tense, annoyed.

"Of course."

The voices of children floated across the hall. Lunch was now officially underway. Cammy J turned and studied the scene. She'd assumed that the clients would mostly be black. They were mostly white, a few native American, and just one black family, a mother and three children. One was a girl with her hair in corn rows. *It must take hours to do*, Cammy J thought. She'd never thought about having children of her own, yet seeing that little girl sitting no nicely in her chair, waiting while the rest of her family served themselves from the bowls on the table, made her heart ache.

"Tell you what. Walk around a bit, get a feel for the place. Then we'll talk specifics. Leave your purse there," Andrea said, and indicated an empty cubby on the wall behind Cammy J.

Cammy J hesitated.

"It'll be safe, don't worry. No thieves here," Andrea said.

Cammy J crossed the hall and took the empty chair next to the little girl. She, her mother, and the two siblings—both boys—stopped eating and stared at Cammy J.

"Hi," Cammy J said.

The mother nodded. Her face was lined. Her eyes were sharp and knowing. She wore a bright headscarf and small gold hoop earrings. Her sweatshirt was stained, though the children's clothes were clean.

"Have you been here long?" Cammy J asked, aware that her tone was overly pleasant.

"Dey just start servin'," the mother said. Her sweatshirt was several sizes too big for her, Cammy J saw.

"I mean how long have you been at the shelter?"

The woman shrugged. "Been awhile. Might get us a new place soon." She continued eating what appeared to be a stew of some sort. The children also ate.

"What's your name?" Cammy J asked the little girl.

"Marcelle."

"Don't talk with yo mouth full," the mother told her. Marcelle swallowed her food.

"I'm sorry. I should let you finish your lunch," Cammy J said.

No one spoke. One of the boys swung his legs, making the table jiggle.

"You cut that out," the mother said. Her voice was flat. She pushed her half-eaten bowl toward the older of the two boys, who'd consumed his serving. Then she watched as he shoveled in spoonful after spoonful.

She's still hungry, Cammy J thought.

"Can I get you anything? Some coffee?" Cammy J asked.

"You new, ain't ya?"

"Yes. Today's my first day."

"Bet it's yo last un, too."

Cammy J flushed. She stood up. "I'll be around, if you need anything," she said, and walked off.

For the next half hour or so, she wandered through the shelter. There were four large dormitories with lockers along one wall and a common area with children's toys, rocking chairs, and a small television set. For privacy, the cots were inside cubicles. Unoccupied ones had folded linens and a single pillow. Those in use were usually unmade, with the sheets often trailing to the floor. Cammy made up one cot, then a second. While doing the third, the person using it, a teenage girl with a tattoo of a spike across her throat, arrived and asked Cammy J what she thought she was doing.

"Just straightening up," Cammy J said.

"I don't need a maid."

"No, of course not."

Cammy J continued her tour. The bathroom offered a row of ten shower stalls on one side and ten sinks on the other. Toilets were in a separate room next door. Everything looked clean, yet dismal, minimal, barely enough somehow. The place was full of people, yet no one spoke to her as she meandered along. When some children ran noisily down the hall, Cammy J stood back and let them pass. A woman, clearly their parent, shouted after them to slow down. Then she looked at Cammy J.

"Why didn't you grab them?" she asked her.

"I don't think I'm allowed to."

"Great. And me, slow as a turtle."

The woman's pale skin had ugly red spots. Her

hair was patchy. She was fat and wheezy. She took a minute to catch her breath, then went on her way.

Cammy J realized she was hungry, and found the kitchen next to the cafeteria. It was huge, with stainless steel everywhere. A skinny black man was mopping the floor.

"Lunch over," he informed her when she asked if there was anything to eat.

"Oh."

"Vending machine got candy."

Cammy J went to the office and found her purse where she'd left it. Her wallet held no coins. The smallest bill she had was a twenty, and she was sure no vending machine could change it. She'd have asked Andrea what to do, but she'd stepped out.

Cammy J was exhausted. She returned to the dormitories, found an empty, unused cot in a vacant cubicle, and lay down. She focused on the sounds around her, which were minimal just then. Maybe it was naptime, and all the running little children were doing just as she was, resting and getting sleepy. She felt utterly defeated, and soon fell asleep.

Someone poked her awake. It was the little girl from lunch, Marcelle.

"How come you crying?" she asked.

"What? I'm not crying. I just closed my eyes."

"Yo face all wet."

Cammy J sat up. Sure enough, her cheeks were damp. What had she dreamed that made her cry? She had no idea. She didn't even know you could cry in your sleep. But once, as a child, she'd laughed in her sleep, or so her mother said, so it must be possible to cry, too.

"You better get back to your mother," Cammy J said.

"She all right. She playin' cards with my brothers."

Cammy J sat up and patted Marcelle's corn rows. Their ridges resisted her touch. She walked Marcelle back to her family, where they were gathered around a table, intently bent over their hands. One boy put down the seven of clubs. His mother smiled and shook her head. Then both boys smiled. Cammy J watched them until the mother looked up and caught her eye.

"You sittin' in?" she asked Cammy J.

Cammy J said she didn't want to be a bother.

"We playin' hearts," said one of the boys. "You don't know it, I teach you."

"You good at dat, too," the mother told him. Then she threw her arm around his neck and squeezed.

"No, really, I don't want to intrude." Cammy J lightly brushed Marcelle's shoulder and turned away. She collected her purse from her cubby and left the building.

Neither Lizzie nor her mother called to ask how her first day had been, because she hadn't told either she was volunteering. She could tell them both now, of course. But they'd want to know how it went, and if she'd go back again in the morning.

That night she wrote: *It's not just money that divides us, or opportunity or access to a better future. Something more splits us into the haves and have-nots.*

Love.

Those that have it are truly blessed. Those who lack it will always hunger for it.

She couldn't post it. The responses would be unbearable.

She sat until her computer's energy saver darkened the screen and cloaked her words.

So this is what it feels like to be trapped and cut off. This is how it is, on the wrong side of the divide.

The emptiness of her past met the greater emptiness ahead. She chewed her thumb, as she'd always done when overcome with grief.

She sat a bit longer, then brought her screen back to life. Her new blog post had taken shape.

anne leigh parrish

She called it "Poverty of The Worst Kind."

the fall

Suicides shot up that winter. By Valentine's Day there'd been four. The victims walked out when the light was low, usually in late afternoon, say three or four o'clock. They stood by the rail (*Josh Skinner, age 21, Indianapolis, Indiana*, or *Lisa Finklestein, age 19, Nassau County, New York*) and waited while their classmates went by head-bent against the rising wind, lugging their textbooks home. Lugging their own heavy hearts, too, or so it was generally accepted, given the highly competitive nature of an Ivy League school. Then, when the crowd had thinned or was gone altogether, they jumped into the gorge. Not all went down in waking hours, though. Some crept out in the freezing night. One (*Louis Kennedy, age 22, Santa Barbara, California*) was found in his pajamas. He must have been so miserable, so intent on self-destruction, that even the deep cold couldn't change his mind.

Kirsten's study group lost interest in their Intro. to Econ. class and focused on the deaths.

"They're like a cult," Emily said. "They need a name. How about the plungers?"

"That's a plumber's tool," Lee said.

"The divers, then."

They all thought of bronzed cliff divers piercing the surface of a calm, sky-blue sea.

Lee wanted another pitcher of beer and offered to pay for it himself. Lee's father sent him money whenever he asked for it, which was often. His offer was quickly accepted.

"Look, we better study for the midterm," Kirsten said.

"We are. We're maximizing our utility," Tom said. His bushy red hair made him seem like someone you couldn't take seriously, Kirsten thought, though he clearly was a serious person.

"Or, we're capturing economies of scale," Lee said. He looked bleary. He wasn't a practiced drinker and wanted to be. He talked about drinking as if it were a sport, something you could win or lose at.

"To stand there, waiting," Emily said. "That's the moment your life changes."

"Bull," Tom said. "The moment your life changes is the moment it ends. The point of impact."

"What about the fall?" Lee asked. "Because then you know it's all over."

"Okay, then, the fall, too. That long, long drop." Tom lifted his hand and sailed it slowly down, back and forth, more like an autumn leaf floating to earth, Kirsten thought, than a body hurtling a hundred feet below.

The beer arrived and was poured out.

"No. It all happens before, when you first consider killing yourself. That's the moment things change," Emily said.

Emily wore nothing but black and pulled her red hair up in a bun so tight the skin by her eyes pulled up, too, giving her an Asiatic look. She had a reckless streak. Sometimes she drank too much, and went to bed with the wrong men, yet she kept up her studies, out of deference to her father. She was a good student, better than the rest of them. Kirsten was jealous of her for that. Kirsten struggled to get a B average. She sipped her beer. She didn't like beer, and drank it for the sake of going along.

"Can we change the subject?" Lee asked.

Kirsten wished they would. For several nights, she had dreamed of falling, but never of hitting earth. In one dream, she willed herself not to fall, but to rise, and that was terrifying, too.

"But think about it," Emily said. "Let's say you go to the bridge, you want to jump, you're ready to, then you change your mind."

"And?" Lee asked.

"You go home. It never happened. You didn't jump and you didn't die. No one else would ever know. But you know. You'd always know how close you came. You'd be changed after that. How could you not be?"

"So, you're saying that wanting to do something and actually doing it are the same thing," Lee said.

"Yes."

"So, our whole lives come down to what we feel—what we desire—whether there's any physical outcome or not."

"Right."

"Wait," Tom said. "Wanting to kill someone isn't the same as actually doing it."

"Or wanting to die and actually dying," Kirsten added.

She pulled her sweaty fingers through her hair. She'd just had it cut in a page boy style that even she had to admit looked like shit. The others had noticed, naturally, but said little. Emily, though, had taken her own hair out of its tight bun and let it drape around her skinny face and shoulders before lifting it once more from her neck. No doubt a way of saying, *I still possess what you gave away!* Before the cut, Kirsten's hair had been long enough to sit on. The change was dramatic, and in the moments before the girl's scissors had closed down, the moment before the first handful had hit the floor, Kirsten, in a panic, forced herself to say nothing and remember that hair, unlike lost lives, will return.

*

The bar was quiet. Tom, Lee, and Emily occupied their usual booth, fourth from the right by the game room, where two townies were shooting pool and not saying a word to each other.

Kirsten had begged off, down with a cold, Emily said. Tom felt he was closer to her than Emily was, and didn't see why Kirsten hadn't called him to cancel.

"She failed," Emily said.

"What?" Lee asked.

"The midterm. Kirsten failed it. She told me when she called. She said that was another reason not to come today, because she obviously wasn't getting anything out of the group."

"Weird," Tom said. He was worried about her. She'd been growing distant and quiet, even before the exam. When the group began last fall, she would laugh a lot. Tom could see she was nervous and trying not to be. Then she stopped laughing as the end of term approached. After the winter break, she came back looking haunted, as if she were listening to something no one else could hear.

Emily shrugged. They drank their beer, opened

their textbooks, then closed them again. They'd all aced the same exam Kirsten failed, and it was as if they'd all come to the same conclusion at the same moment—they didn't need to study so hard.

"What's the deal with her hair, anyway?" Lee asked. "Major chop job."

"Looks like she did it herself," Emily said.

"No way. Really?" Tom asked.

"Sure. I can see her standing there in front of her mirror, going at it with rusty shears."

"Why rusty?"

"Oh, I don't know. There's just something decayed about her."

Tom felt bad again. He didn't like Emily. She was arrogant and cruel, but what she'd said about Kirsten was true.

*

The Econ. exam was one of three Kirsten failed. She was up to speed in her American History course, but when she opened the exam book to write the essay, she froze. Her mind ran down one path, then up another. Words raced through, and she couldn't capture them, or even slow them down. Geology was a multiple choice, and what tripped her up there was a sudden obsession with filling in the ovals completely—perfectly—with no lead outside the line. The moment she finished one she checked it again and again. She erased several answers to start over from scratch, and when time was called, she'd completed less than half the test. Her failures took air out of whatever room she was in. She went to the health clinic. "I've got asthma," she told the nurse. A doctor listened hard to her breathing, and disagreed. He asked if she was getting enough rest. "Well, you know, we just finished midterms." He said to go and catch up on her sleep.

In her Econ. lecture, she moved to the back, away from Emily, Lee, and Tom. Tom turned back sometimes and smiled at her. The others didn't. One day he caught up with her in the hall. She'd tried to escape and wasn't fast enough.

"Hey," Tom said. "You have time for a beer?"

She pulled back, against the wall, and hugged her backpack as if it were a stuffed bear.

"Sure," she said, breaking out in a sweat.

"How are things?" Tom asked.

"Fine."

They left the building. Their path took them over the gorge. Kirsten walked on the outside, away from the railing. The sunshine was painful. Tom put on a pair of sunglasses. He looked like a movie star, she thought. Like someone important.

"We miss you in the study group," he said.

"I bet you don't. At least, Emily and Lee don't."

"Who cares about them? You should come back. If you think you want to, that is."

"I don't think I'd get much out of it. Besides, I've got a part-time job now, well, a volunteer job, really, and I won't be around as much."

"Really? Where are you volunteering?"

"The counseling center."

Kirsten had never been into the counseling center, but she'd seen a flyer asking for volunteers. *Are you good with people? Do you have time to listen? No special training necessary. Call today to attend an orientation session.*

With two beers in her, Kirsten relaxed a little. For some reason, for the moment she felt safe.

"We should go out some time," Tom said.

"We're out right now."

"I mean at night."

"You mean, like a date?"

"Why not?"

"Okay."

But Tom got busy with school again and didn't ask Kirsten for a date.

*

The moment she walked into the counseling center, Kirsten knew she'd done the right thing. The potted plants were lush. Tropical. One was red and leafy. Later she realized they were plastic, and wasn't disappointed. Keeping a foreign thing like that alive in the Dunston air—even heated air—would be hard. Yet, when she'd first seen the town the spring before, after she'd been admitted, having applied sight unseen, she found it full of life. Lots of thick green trees and deer off in the roadside woods. Growing up in Los Angeles meant both trees and deer were scarce. She hoped—at times she was dead certain—that coming to school there would mean a much needed renewal. Her own life taking shape and rounding out.

Her father wanted her to go to Stanford, because he had. Though he knew she wanted to escape the house he'd spent his whole life building, and the wife/mother he'd spent years trying to improve, the moment never came when he could admit it to her. "Do us proud" was all he said. Kirsten's mother was devastated. They had never been close, yet she couldn't bear being left alone with a man who thought she was his doormat. The mother knew her own weakness, her failure to take hold of her own life, had passed on to the daughter, who was equally meek. Yet there was a sliver of steel in her somewhere, her mother was sure. The question was where, and what would cause it to break the surface?

Kirsten was shown to an African-American man who sat at a dusty desk. An ivy plant trailed to the floor. It looked real. Her touch confirmed it. She was confused. The fake plants were in front, and the living ones were in back. Which meant you progressed from death to life, when it was really the other way around. If not, that meant—

"Pray," the man said

"What?"

"Name's Pray." He pointed to a piece of wood on his desk.

"Odd name."

"Even before I was born, my mother was convinced my soul needed saving."

"Did it?"

"I've been pretty good so far, but it's too soon to tell."

His teeth were very white. The dreadlocks she wasn't sure about. She'd always thought they looked stupid.

"So, what can I do for you?" he asked.

"I'd like to volunteer."

"That's great. Why would you like to volunteer here, as opposed to say, an animal shelter?"

Was he baiting her?

"Because people seem to be in trouble," she said. "The stress seems to be building up."

"That's probably true. Well, Kirsten, why don't you tell me a little bit about yourself?"

It was like talking about someone else. Growing up in Brentwood, coming to the Ivy League to study—what, she wasn't sure. Maybe theater, though she was terrified of performing; so maybe history, though the relevance of that wasn't always clear because all of us, even historians, had to live in the moment, didn't they?; so maybe economics, since that seemed to be what made the world go around— the trouble was she'd just failed her exam, and the grade report had already been sent home, and she could just imagine how it would be received. Her father could ooze disappointment like pus from a wound (she then apologized for her choice of words).

She talked more. It got easier. There were so many random points in her life, all these things off the side, like how her aunt tried to show her how to paint once and got fed up with her, or how she'd fallen in love with a palomino pony her father said was too much responsibility for her, or how her piano teacher once told her she was probably wasting her time. She told Pray she thought she was supposed to connect all the points somehow, like the picture puzzles kids used to do, because she was sure there was something underneath all the dots, if she could only get far enough away to really look down and see it.

Pray told her she should make an appointment with one of the counselors there. She thought he meant so she could learn what to tell people who came in, at the end of their rope.

"It never hurts to explore these feelings in a safe environment," he said.

The moment she realized he thought she was nuts, she stood up and left.

*

The snow came on hard. A March snow was supposed to have less force, or so she'd been told. Or had she ever been told what snow was supposed to do, and if so, when? Kirsten's roommate spent all her time at her boyfriend's frat, leaving Kirsten on her own. It was better that way. Celia, the roommate, talked a lot and wore perfume that made Kirsten's throat itch. The moment she left, taking the scent with her, Kirsten stopped coughing.

The snow fell for two days and three nights, and on the morning of the third day the world had become visible once more, and blindingly bright. All the sunlight in Southern California was nothing compared to this, yet Kirsten didn't mind squinting her way across the main quad, across the gorge where icicles hung like huge teeth, around the athletic center, past the physics building, along the edge of College Town, then back to her dorm. She hadn't attended any of her classes for ten days. When that time reached a total of two weeks, a letter would be mailed home, or so the student handbook had said. Her father had suffered the grade report in silence, but she was sure the letter would prompt a telephone call, or worse, his appearance at her door. But no, he wouldn't waste his time coming all that way to fetch her back. He'd tell her to get on the next plane home. He'd make himself scarce when she did return, avoiding conversation, avoiding her, avoiding, avoiding, avoiding. Her mother wouldn't meet her eye, and then one morning, Kirsten would awaken to find her sitting on the end of her bed, watching her sleep.

She couldn't go home. Not after submitting herself so easily to failure. She'd have to stay right there in Dunston, and suffer it out, moment by moment.

Her room felt too small, even with Celia gone. She moved Celia's dresser into the hall, wrestled her desk out there, too, and stripped her bed. The R.A. asked what she was doing. Kirsten explained.

198

"You can't do that. This room is assigned as a double. Everything has to go back the way it was."

Kirsten promised to replace the furniture. She locked the door. The room still felt small. She tore down the curtains and hoped the light would widen everything it fell on. It didn't. She needed a shower. She hadn't had one for four days. The sight of her own nakedness had become disturbing. There were too many mirrors in the bathroom. She thought they should be painted black to spare her having to see herself. She gathered what she needed—shampoo, soap, a towel that stank of mildew because she'd never once put it through the laundry, different clothes, none of them clean—and made her way into the bathroom. She turned off the light. Without windows, she stood in total darkness. *This is what the blind experience all the time.* That was both fascinating and terrifying. She inched toward the shower stall, put her things just outside it on the floor, and slid her hand along the cold, smooth tile until she found the lever that turned on the water. She stripped. She found her soap and shampoo, and got into the stall. As she was rinsing her hair, the light went on.

"What the fuck are you doing taking a shower in the dark?" The voice belonged to a fat girl two doors down. Kirsten had never learned her name. She didn't answer.

"Oh, and you might want to close the curtain."

Kirsten saw that she'd soaked the clothes she'd intended to wear because there'd been nothing to block the water. She pushed down the lever, wrapped herself in her wet towel, gathered her belongings, then returned to her room and wept.

*

Tom knocked on her door. He smelled of fresh air and the Indian food he'd had for lunch. His presence made the room warm.

"You look like shit, if you don't mind my saying so," he said. His backpack hit the floor.

"I'm fine."

"Have you been sick?"

"No. Just working hard."

"You haven't been in class."

"I needed some time off."

He sat down on the end of her bed. She'd been sleeping in a sleeping bag on the floor. When she heard the knock, she'd kicked the bag under the bed.

"You look like you could use some fresh air," he said. "Let's go for a walk."

"It's freezing."

"It'll do you good."

200

They sat, not talking for a while. As he was leaving, he hugged her. She didn't understand why. She felt his heartbeat through his T-shirt, and flannel shirt, and the sweater he wore over all of that, and the heavy coat on the outside. How could that be? How could anyone's heart be that strong?

The moment the door closed behind him, the room rushed outwards, spreading like a stain. That's stupid, she thought. It's just a room.

*

The hour was late. She'd been up all night for the second day straight. She was hungry. A candy bar from the vending machine downstairs would really hit the spot, and then the thought turned her stomach. Tom had called twice. She hadn't answered. If she saw him, she'd say her phone had run down. *Out of juice*, she'd say. *Like a squeezed orange.*

Then the moment came when she could no longer stand the confines of her room. She dressed in layers. Ice crystals lay on the black window, brightened here and there by the street lamp three floors below. Outside, the paths were black and the snow was white, but a dim white, as if the life and power had been drained from it.

Snow that lay in darkness must have a name, she

thought. Night snow? But its color. What was the color, exactly? Were colors exact or approximate? Was this something she was supposed to know? Did anyone know?

Too many questions and not enough answers. That was her problem. How could she go through life in this state of constant ignorance? Was that why people ended it, because there were too many things they didn't know? Or, was it knowing that they'd never find out? And seeing that death was the one big mystery, the one thing no one really knew for sure, they hastened it, rushed into it, all for that desperate need to know.

Her boots were silent as they hit the ground. No one was out. The world had gone completely still. The only thing moving was the silver plume of her own breath. She heard the water in the gorge well before she reached the bridge. The sound was like a song of defiance, because the water was stronger than the cold. The water did not freeze.

She felt nothing. Not the bitter air. Not fear. Not regret. She'd stopped thinking about the people she'd once known, how they would take her end, what their lives would be like as they moved forward without her.

The railing was under construction. Renovation, actually. A barrier was being placed that would prevent climbers from being able to jump unless they snuck by at either end. She stood there, aware of the challenge, but also of a change in the light around her. It was growing brighter. Dawn was underway. She'd never been awake at dawn before, never seen the sunrise. The first and last, she thought, then felt the idea was trite.

Then the light rose enough so that an icicle hanging from a dark ledge of shale was illuminated. It seemed to glow. Kirsten had never seen anything so beautiful. She didn't understand how the light had reached the ice before falling on anything else. Soon other icicles were coming to life, turning a faint, warm yellow.

"My God," she said, holding the rail with her gloved hands.

"Are you all right?" a man's voice asked. She turned. All there was of him was his thick coat and wool hat. He asked the question again.

"Look at the gorge. Look at the light. Isn't it amazing?"

The man turned. He didn't seem to know what she was talking about.

"It's damn early to be up and about," he said.

"It's beautiful."

"I work on campus. I have to be there by six.

That's why I'm out here freezing my ass off."

She said nothing.

"What are you doing out here, if you don't mind my asking?" he asked.

Suddenly, she no longer knew. She was cold. And tired and very hungry. She continued to look at the icicles and realized the man wasn't going to walk off until she went, too. She gazed down, hearing the water rush, held by the dawn, feeling as if she herself were lit from within.

bree's miracle

Bree had a female complaint. Bad periods, I mean this girl could really bleed. Started at age eleven, would probably be pushing sixty when she quit, lots and lots of Advil on board, not to mention all the Kotex she could run through in that wretched week a month. And the pain, can you imagine?

Her doctor told her she had a fibroid. She stared at him over her raised knees. A non-cancerous growth, he said. Completely harmless. Except that it caused excessive bleeding, which is why she tended to be anemic and why her periods were so agonizing. She missed work because of them. Her boss was not very sympathetic. He suspected her of malingering.

The doctor looked at her over his bifocals, assessing her in some way that wasn't purely medical. He suggested an ultrasound to get a better look at the thing. The procedure was explained.

The ultrasound required that her bladder be full. Really full. About to burst full. Bree considered downing a bunch of beer and thought that might not be wise. She drank four glasses of water during the course of one hour, then drove to the clinic where the procedure would be performed. She signed in, and hopped lightly from one foot to another to keep from peeing in her pants. The receptionist was unmoved.

She was no doubt quite accustomed to women walking on tiptoes, knees together, with gritted teeth and tense faces.

The bed Bree lay in was remarkably comfortable. It was wide, and the head lifted at the press of a button. Her grandmother had a bed like that in her home, for which she'd paid a handsome price. She was very fond of elevating her feet because her ankles tended to swell. Bree was unsure whether this particular bed also had a foot lift. She was about to ask, when the ultrasound technician inserted the probe between Bree's legs and focused hard on the screen.

He was silent as he worked, though his gaze grew more and more alarmed. Bree tried to remain calm. The technician excused himself for a moment, told Bree she could use the bathroom if she needed to, and said he'd be right back. Bree scurried from the table and walked, bent over, to the adjacent room. She was on the toilet a good forty-five seconds. When she was empty at last, her sense of alarm rose up again. What had the technician seen that upset him so?

When she returned, the technician and her doctor were seated together before the monitor, looking at the images frozen there. The doctor asked Bree to take a seat on the bed for the time being.

"I have no explanation for this, but your fibroid

has the face of the Virgin Mary," he said.

"Get out," Bree said, weak with relief that her plight was not at all serious.

"I'm telling you the truth. You have received a remarkable and mysterious blessing."

The doctor turned the monitor around so that Bree could view the image for herself. It was the Virgin, all right—head bent, expression demur, halo charmingly tilted.

"Is the baby Jesus there with her?" Bree asked. She still wasn't able to take any of this seriously.

The doctor appeared stunned by her question. He told the technician to re-insert the probe and take more pictures.

"But I just emptied my bladder," Bree said. The doctor didn't care. Even without the pressure of all that urine, an image of Jesus—if it were truly there— would come through clearly.

And, it did.

The doctor crossed himself, and then said he wasn't a religious man. Bree was witness to a conversion. Miracle upon miracle, in that tiny room.

"What about the fibroid? It *is* a fibroid, right?" Bree asked.

"No doubt about it. A most glorious, special fibroid."

"I still want it removed," Bree said.

"You can't be serious! You've been handed a miracle, and you wish to destroy it?"

The technician was glaring at her now, too.

"Hey, guys, take a chill pill," Bree said. "Let's not forget that this is my body we're talking about here. Plus, it hurts like hell. I want the damn thing out."

The doctor shook his head sadly.

The trouble with women, he said, is that they don't understand that simply to be a woman is to be supremely blessed.

"You are givers of life. You are duty-bound to preserve it," he said.

"It's a fucking fibroid!"

Bree swung her legs from the table. She told the two men in the room to give her a moment to dress. Then she met the doctor back in his office to further discuss the situation.

The doctor implored her to reconsider.

No way. She wanted it gone.

He could not support that decision.

Then she'd find a doctor who would.

How could he make her see that she was in the hands of something larger?

There was nothing larger, or more important.

208

"If you were a woman, you'd understand," Bree said.

She left him sitting at his desk, clearly in a state of woe.

The doctor she found to rid her of her affliction was pleasant, efficient, and said that it was very refreshing to meet a young woman who knew her own mind.

"The world needs more like you," he said.

Bree couldn't agree more.

Afterwards, she never had a moment's regret about doing away with the Virgin Mary and the baby Jesus, who had, for some insane reason, decided to make a home in her womb.

patience

Patience was misnamed. Rage, Anger, or Wrath would have been more apt. Clearly her mother was in an optimistic frame of mind when she chose what to call her unwanted, unplanned, and unusual child. That her existence came as a surprise didn't mean love was withheld. Patience was cared for, tended, never shunned. As she grew, it was her mother who wished to possess the quality she'd named her child. Patience was difficult, rambunctious, seldom at ease with her own skin.

Her teachers were the first to sound the alarm. Patience was perfectly intelligent, they said, but showed no interest in learning. She seemed to have contempt for the whole process. Patience declared to her baffled mother that the teachers in the Snow school across the road gave their students homework. They had class trips and assemblies.

How Patience knew this was unclear. Snow people didn't mingle with Mud people. They kept to themselves, and Patience's people were expected to do the same.

"No point in worrying what goes on over there," her mother said. "It's not for you, or me, or any of us."

"Why not? I'm just as good as they are!"

"Because. It's always been that way."

"Then I'll cross the road. I'll go to that school. I'll learn what the Snow kids learn."

"Patience, no! You must not cross that road! Snow and Mud don't mix!"

What bothered Patience was that her people did cross the road. They went every day to clean houses, iron sheets, cook, and take away a few coins and bills placed on whatever surface was near—a counter, the top of a barrel—but never into the hand, for snow must not touch mud.

Snow can melt, and mud can harden, Patience thought. It was Patience herself who hardened, but only on the inside. Outwardly, she seemed to have adopted a spirit of quiet resignation which pleased her mother to no end.

Time passed, as time always does, and things changed for the Mud and Snow people. A new spirit of cooperation and acceptance seemed to prevail. Snow people and Mud people became friends, business partners, even lovers. Sometimes they married. A new identity seemed to be at hand, and Patience, now a community leader, sought a new vocabulary—a new name. Mud people were descended from the earth, the rich ground from which food came, and Patience advocated being called Children of the Soil. When that was too long,

211

and thus inconvenient, it was shortened to Soil. Snow people wanted a name change, too, and since snow fell from above, they became Sky.

For a while, everyone was happy with their new names. Then trouble started again because Soil was always lower than Sky. Patience tried to impress upon the citizens of her town that both were equally necessary to survival, and so both should be treated equally under the law. Patience was older, her hair was streaked with white. Yet her passion for justice was as strong as ever.

While the law came to recognize equality, the hearts of human beings did not. Soil was still considered less valuable than Sky. And because the peacekeepers were usually Sky, further trouble ensued. Rights, once briefly respected, were ignored. Young Soil men, unarmed, were shot by Sky police who later swore that they believed a weapon had been in hand. One horrible mistake could be explained as simple human error. But the trend continued. Soil feared; Sky reigned.

In a city by the river that cut the country in two, a young Soil man walked down a street. The street appealed to him. It was open and wide. Traffic was light; he wasn't concerned for his safety. The day was warm; the world felt gentle. Until a Sky police officer drove up and told him to stop walking in the road.

"Is there a law against walking in the road?" Soil asked Sky.

The officer repeated his request. His voice grew loud. The world wasn't gentle. A final command was issued, a shot fired, a Soil man was now down in the street. The Sky officer claimed self-defense. The Soil man charged him, clearly intending to do him harm! Certainly he'd had a weapon, if not in plain sight, then concealed somewhere on his person. No weapon could be found, though, and the Soil community raged.

Patience brought her people together. They held a vigil. They sang. They walked arm in arm to the Sky police precinct, where they were met with two Soil police officers, who knew that they were tokens, yet acquitted themselves with honor and respect. The crowd was allowed to remain in place, singing, taking turns speaking at the podium that had been set up at the suggestion of the mayor. He promised a full investigation. He assured them that the matter would be handled fairly.

Patience knew there was no fairness. Her people knew it, too. They spoke of retaliation, of causing mayhem and strife. They would arm themselves in protest, and for their own protection. Patience counseled against it. Only greater anguish would result.

Night fell. Patience tied up her hair. She washed her hands and feet. She put on a clean white dress and a necklace which had belonged to her long dead mother, a string of amber stones separated by silver balls, the only thing of value Patience owned.

She prayed. *Let me end better than I began; let me die better than I lived.*

The pavement was cool against her bare feet. She entered the street where the Soil man had been slain. On its surface were the invisible footprints of her people as they'd walked together in song. She walked on and on in the night. The police car approached her slowly, its lights dancing in the dark. The voice commanded her to stop and to come no closer. She raised her hands, walked on, waiting for the sound of gunfire, then willing it to come.

fire and ice

They sat on six acres, so there was plenty of room. And since getting laid off, he had plenty of time. When the cement plant was hiring again, he'd gotten a phone call from Dodd, his supervisor there for over fifteen years. Clarence said no thank you, he was doing just fine in retirement. Sandy needed a second cup of coffee for that one. Clarence was forty-seven years old. Who the hell retires at forty-seven? Especially with five years left on the mortgage and the salary from her job with the school district not exactly plush?

Sandy's mother advised her to button her lip.

"The man's in bad shape," she said.

Sandy knew all about his bad shape. The hunting accident had happened over four years before, but Clarence was in those damned woods every day, walking silently as he'd been taught to do by his own father, waiting for the buck, holding perfectly still, taking his time, then very gently squeezing the trigger of his father's old Winchester .30-06. Poor Lucas had to get his ass in the line of fire at the wrong moment. Well, not his ass, his left arm, which was probably better since he was right-handed, not that he used either hand for anything gainful, living off his little sister his whole adult life. Lucas was in the hospital for a while, learning how to deal with a shattered humerus, enjoying the morphine and the kindly touch of his nurses.

Really, he'd taken the whole thing a lot better than Clarence had. Lucas was proud of his arm's gnarly surgical scar, even of its shrunken muscles, and the way it dangled by his side while he gestured wildly with the other one.

No matter how many times Sandy told Clarence that things could have been a whole lot worse, because after all Lucas was alive and well, he got all dark and distant.

And then the lay-off came. While Sandy put pencil to paper and figured out how they were going to make it on his unemployment and her salary, Clarence sat in front of the television set with the sound off, his feet on the coffee table, arms folded across his round stomach. When he looked up from the screen, he seemed not to recognize his surroundings.

He needed to pull out of himself. So it was ironic that the vehicle for that action was Lucas, the one who'd shoved him down inside in the first place.

Lucas' 1980 Buick Le Sabre had a bad carburetor, which he'd rebuilt four times already. Maybe his funky arm and hand made the job harder, or maybe it was because he'd always been a few bricks short of a load anyway, but he just couldn't get it to work. So, Clarence told him they'd go out to the junk yard and look for a replacement.

The junk yard was under new management. Clarence didn't know Foster had sold out. The boy behind the counter told him so. Not much of a boy, really, at well over six feet when he stood, with the tattoo of a dagger on his forearm. What threw Clarence, but not so much Lucas (because Lucas had a bunch of weirdness in his life), was that the guy was knitting a baby sweater with tiny needles. Doing it well, too, as far as Clarence could tell. Sandy was a knitter, sometimes. The boy, Glen, explained that his wife was expecting and had wanted to knit a bunch of sweaters and hats and booties for the coming winter but she had very bad arthritis, the kind you get when you're a kid, so Glen said he'd learn and do it for her. His mother showed him how, then asked him flat out if he had a thing in general for girlie stuff. He wasn't offended. It seemed like a fair question. He liked to knit, he realized, but it made him reluctant to handle auto parts, on account of the grease and grime, so the customers did their own picking and carrying.

Clarence digested this information and said what he was looking for. Glen nodded. The GM's were in row three, more or less. His dad—the new owner—had been trying to get the place organized. That guy Foster had a screw loose when it came to order, but that made sense, didn't it, owning a junk yard? "Get it? screw loose? old cars?" Glen put his knitting in his lap and laughed until his face turned red and his eyes watered. Clarence had to hand it to him; being able to crack yourself up was a worthy talent.

Clarence and Lucas made their way down the wide, dusty row. The drought was in its fourth month. Burns, Oregon, was naturally dry anyway, and now it was even drier. Clarence wanted to move somewhere wet, with sixty inches of rain a year, like the Olympic Peninsula, maybe, or the east side of any island in Hawaii. He used to have quite a thing for geography when he was a kid. He'd picked up a lot from his mother's old books. He didn't figure he'd be able to talk Sandy into moving. She didn't love her job, but she was very dedicated to it. She was the secretary for the whole school district. Okay, it had maybe four hundred students in it, but someone had to keep all the paperwork straight, and that was her.

After forty-five minutes, no Le Sabre was to be had, so they took the carburetor out of a Monte Carlo instead. Although the Le Sabre had a bigger engine, a V-8 versus a V-6, Lucas was pretty sure the carb would work. And it did. Lucas was delighted.

Clarence wasn't. He was agitated. Something had woken up inside him, and wasn't being at all quiet about it. He'd never been one to believe much in second chances, but his was staring right at him. He wanted to bring old cars back to life, thereby bestowing a second chance upon them, too.

Sandy said a hobby was fine, a hobby was good, as long as it didn't end up costing them a lot of money. Clarence removed his baseball cap and scratched the back of his head. Clearly, the thought of money hadn't occurred to him. Salvage cars were cheap, not free. He begged her to take a closer look at the books and see if there was a little funny money he could have. Sandy brewed another pot of coffee and stood, listening to it drip. Clarence had three more months of unemployment coming. He could use half of it. That was the best she could do.

The first was a 1975 Camaro. He got his buddy Brewster to tow it home for free. Brewster didn't have much to tow in the summer. Winter was when everyone broke down or skidded into ditches, so he was glad for something to do.

The wreck itself only set Clarence back seventy-five dollars. In good condition, the car would have been a collector's item, but it was missing both bumpers and the passenger seat. And the radio. And the back lights. It lacked a windshield, too. Clarence listed all these drawbacks in his head while he circled it lovingly on the dead swath of grass where Sandy once had had a flower garden.

Every morning he was up to beat the midday heat. He took things off and put them back on. He went again and again to the junk yard, prowled the rows looking for what he needed. Sometimes he found it. Usually he didn't. Glen was still knitting. He'd stopped making baby clothes and was working on a scarf for his dad.

After a week and a half, Clarence gave up on the Camaro and was jonesing for a sweet little Ford Galaxy. It had no steering wheel, but the leather seats were intact. So were two of its whitewall tires. The paint must once have been red. It was impossible to tell. He got it for a song because Glen had just taken a phone call from his wife. His side of the conversation made it clear that some medical issue had come up, and he was clearly worried. He let the Galaxy go for fifty.

By the first week of September, roughly nine weeks from the time the first injured car had made its appearance on their property, there were six rusting carcasses outside Sandy's kitchen window. Clarence spent every daylight hour, even in the heat, under them, inside them, on top of them, poking, prodding, in an obscene display of affection that bordered on sexual.

There was fire in his eyes and a cool steadiness in his hands. Even the way he sat on the porch when the day was done and watched the sun sink beyond the distant rise spoke of man standing firmly in the center of his own heart.

After another week, Sandy was back at work, using the ancient computer system to update enrollment records, vaccination records, absenteeism among both students and teachers, and the roster of licensed substitutes. Then she met with the head of the PTSA, a toad of a woman named Emeline Dorn, about her plans for fall fundraising. This was an annual headache because residents of Harney County weren't exactly knee-deep in riches. Bake sales, rummage sales, and sending a troupe of sixth-graders door to door with a canned speech about needing to buy new sports equipment (when the District really needed to invest in technology) were going to produce about the same number of dollars that year as in all the years before: somewhere between one hundred and one hundred and fifty. Emeline really wished Sandy could be a little more enthusiastic. Sandy suggested Emeline consult with the principal, Alvin Crockett. Alvin's father-in-law owned the local radio station. Sandy made this suggestion every year, and Emeline acted upon it every year, and every year the principal's wife wrote a check for over a thousand dollars just to make her go away.

In the middle of the second week of school, the new high school science teacher was accused of inappropriately touching Marla Mayvins on the buttocks. The teacher was a young man, in his late twenties, and Marla was fourteen going on thirty. The usual hysterical uproar ensued, and he was put on leave without pay, pending an investigation. Sandy was reminded again how little true justice there was in this world. She'd crossed paths with Marla a number of times over the years because her attendance was so spotty and her mother had no interest in urging Marla to get up in the morning and get on the damned school bus. Why Marla had gone to school that particular day, when the science teacher, Roy Randall, was supposed to have goosed her, was proof that the thread holding all things together was unfair, corrupt, and basically stupid.

It was in this sour mood that Sandy returned home to find that Clarence's latest acquisition was blocking her access to the driveway. She had four bags of groceries to unload. She found him around back, sitting on an iron bench he'd also brought home from the junkyard, drinking a diet Coke, and staring happily into space. He offered to carry the bags in for her, if that would help. What would help is if he got rid of some of these useless relics, called Dodd, and went back to work. The merry light in his eyes turned cold. He was sorry she'd had a bad day but that was no reason to take out her problems on him.

You and those fucking cars are my problem, she almost said. Keeping those words to herself was the most painful thing that had befallen her in a long time. She wished then that she had developed a taste for liquor.

Glen's baby was born, and he took time off to help his wife at home. He told Clarence to take whatever he wanted from the yard, that they'd settle accounts later. Clarence and Brewster transported four more cars and parts of cars, particularly tires which Clarence had become very attached to. Sandy's yard looked like its own salvage operation, and she told Clarence he should go into business for himself. He didn't understand. He didn't bring the cars home so he could resell them. He had them to work on. Only he didn't work on them the way he had. He seemed to have come to the end of his already limited expertise. Sandy said he should look for work at a service station. Maybe one of the guys there could teach him about cars. They were certified mechanics, right? Clarence couldn't possibly mix commerce with art. He hoped she understood. Fine, she said, then call Dodd and see if he'll still take you back. Clarence wasn't ready for Dodd, either.

Another day, Sandy came home to find Clarence welding car parts together. As to what he was making, he couldn't really say. There was just something so beautiful about how the metal could come alive under the heat, bond, and become something else entirely. Sandy felt like she was losing her mind. Roy Randall, the science teacher, had been let go, and Marla Mayvins was playing the downtrodden but plucky victim for all it was worth.

She didn't mean to break down and cry, because she wasn't a crier. But it was just too much. She needed him to help, to earn some money, it didn't matter how. Would he possibly think of selling his pieces? She knew people who did that. One of the English teachers at school crocheted hats for cats. She posted pictures on the internet, and people actually bought them. The cats looked cute with their ears all bundled up. Clarence realized she was coming unglued and brewed a nice strong pot of coffee. As she sat, huddled, still sobbing quietly, he regretted that he wasn't a drinking man.

The weather turned cold. Clarence gave up working on the cars and longed for a large, heated garage. What would it set them back to build one? Sandy didn't answer. The set of her chin said he should probably not bring it up again.

The day that Clarence's last unemployment check arrived, it snowed for the first time that season. Gorgeous fat flakes drifting all around. Sandy usually loved snow and how cozy it made their home feel. Now their home was a trap, with Clarence always in it, doing nothing but silently wishing for what he couldn't have.

She supposed it was inevitable, really. She'd read cases of people who reach the end and become desperate. The spare gas container they kept out back had just about three gallons in it, which was plenty to douse all the cars and parts of cars, though she was careful not to get any on the tires and to actually haul the tires out of reach because she didn't want to smell burning rubber. She also moved the welding equipment, which might have some future value. Clarence had fallen asleep in front of the television when she went out in the twilight with the matches in her pocket. For a moment she wondered if the flames would reach the house, and if so, would she wake Clarence up and drag him to safety?

The noise, smell, and dancing light woke him up. He stood beside her with his hands to his head saying, "What the fuck? What the fuck?"

She told him to shut up and appreciate how pretty it was, the flames and snowfall, like some ancient scene or reckoning. A true clash of opposites, she said. Fire and ice. "Does that make sense?" she asked. He could find no words at the moment, though he agreed wholeheartedly that it made complete and perfect sense.

a thing of beauty

They had to get out of the heat. It was the reason they came, yet after only a day its strength overwhelmed them. Home was dark and wet. Here was bright and dry. The shaded walkway in Oldtown was made of wood that creaked. They were the youngest people around. Arizona was full of retirees, yet there must be plenty of folks under seventy, right?

Nina didn't know. Tom's question made her head hurt a little more. It was the dry air, she thought. The blazing sun. She'd get used to it if she lived there, right? Didn't one always adapt?

"You'll get used to it," her mother had said. At the time, Nina assumed she meant the act of sex, with which she was already quite familiar. Later she knew her mother had meant the married state in general. Living with someone day in, day out.

The store was on a corner. The entrance was guarded by a wooden Indian in a feather headdress. The eyes were painted blue.

"A blue-eyed Indian? What could be more fake than that?" Tom asked.

"A wooden one," Nina said.

The chill from the air conditioning shocked. Nina's breathing slowed. Native goods were

227

everywhere. Moccasins, blankets. Also a horse skull tacked to the wall, kachina dolls, glass cases full of pottery and fetishes. Turquoise jewelry dominated. Large squash blossom necklaces drew her gaze.

A case further along held more modern silver pieces. One, a cuff bracelet, stopped her, pulled her in for a closer look. Against a background of oxidized silver was a pattern of circles, all touching, all linked, none the same size. The other half of the cuff, hinged and held with a tight silver spring, was a mirror image.

Nina asked to see it. She tried it on. It suited her perfectly. Tom said it was too heavy, not right for her. Something smaller, maybe. More delicate.

Nina ignored him. The weight of the bracelet made her feel like a warrior. The girl who opened the case had hair dyed white. Her black eyebrows gave that away. Nina had taken to dying her own hair black. Tom missed her natural red and wanted it back.

Nina paid for the bracelet without considering the impact its cost would have on their budget. Tom would remind her in no time, she was sure. He was good with money because he never spent it. Except when he wanted something, like this vacation. He needed to get away. Work piled up, a woman in his office kept calling him at home. His voice changed when he heard hers. His face did, too. Nina knew the nature of this change, what lay behind it.

They braved the heat once more, but not for long. Tom was hungry. He wanted to sit in the shade with a margarita. He hoped a really good brand of tequila would be on hand. They found a Mexican place, staffed by young men and women with Hispanic features. The man in the open kitchen, which they passed on their way to the cool, lusciously floral back patio, was white.

They sat. A bird with shiny breast feathers stood on the metal rail a few feet away. Nina couldn't fathom its obvious joy. When she brought her glass of white wine to her lips, the new bracelet slid down her arm. She wondered if her joy were obvious, too.

Tom had his margarita. The rim of the glass was salted. Nina had never cared for the taste of salt, but when it wasn't there, she could tell and missed it. How can you miss something you don't really care for? Unless to miss was simply to notice something was gone, something you didn't necessarily want back.

"You like?" Tom asked. She thought he meant the thing of beauty on her wrist. He referred to her wine.

"Yes. The bracelet, too."

"Let me see it."

She extended her arm.

"No, I mean take it off."

She took it off and gave it to him.

In his hand it looked small but no less lovely.

"Rather clever, isn't it?" he asked.

She asked to have the bracelet back. He was still looking at it. He pulled the two halves apart and examined the spring they were welded to. He spread the bracelet further and further open. Nina asked him to stop. She was sure he'd break it. He continued to pull until the pieces could go no further.

Then he released them. They snapped closed. Nina grabbed the bracelet and examined it for damage. There was a tiny nick on one edge, barely visible. It didn't worry her. Silver was a soft metal, and even if Tom hadn't played with it, soon enough there would be small scratches and dents.

"See? Everything comes back together in the end," Tom said.

Nina opened the halves slowly and slipped her narrow wrist into the opening. The halves closed gently. It *was* beautiful, she thought. A gorgeous handcuff.

the lillian girl

Eunice Fitch, age seven, lived in a drafty, clapboard house her parents tried miserably to make a home in. The roof, which sagged under time's weight and ravage, leaked—in Eunice's room, as luck would have it. The plaster softened, yielded, and dripped its steady measure of every passing cloud. Eunice's solution was to get a large pot from the kitchen and push her bed as far back as possible. During a particularly rainy season, when sleep failed to come and the new day began in a ragged state, Eunice moved to a small room at the far end of the hall where the roof, for the time being, held fast.

Her parents often left her alone at night, so they could play cards with another couple down the road. Her companion was the black and white television set in the living room, two floors below the unsound roof. One evening, she was treated to a festival of silent movies. Background music played, piano and strings, cheerful or dire, by turns. Eunice tried to read the lips of the silent movie stars but found herself relying on the subtitles instead. She loved the subtitles. They summed up the action and gave the gist, just enough to go on. She loved the queer lighting, the fabulous twenties gowns, and most of all Lillian Gish. Eunice was enthralled by her courage and beauty.

She sought to perfect the burning gaze, the taut skin around her eyes, the firm jaw. All these conveyed rage, fear, and love from the firmest part of her soul. An elegant display of suffering when she got teased at school after she spilled her milk down the front of her ill-fitting plaid dress. Her reward for this brilliant performance on a spring day full of birdsong was to be called a retard by the tallest boy in class.

Next, she cut her hair in a bob. Her red curls and waves lay gorgeously on the filthy bathroom floor. Her mother was outraged. Several slaps ensued. Her classmates, however, recovered then from the milk disaster, admired her new do. Sadly, she'd done a poor job. The back, in particular, was uneven. And since her hair was so thick and full of body, it stuck up in a way Eunice didn't care for. In the movie that night, *An Unseen Enemy*, Lillian Gish wore her hair long. When she went for the scissors, Eunice realized she had been thinking of another silent star, Clara Bow. Eunice's mother had one treasure to her name, a poster from Bow's 1926 film, *Man Trap*. Eunice had made a stupid mistake.

Thus began a series of misfortunes, all born of a reckless, hungry heart. Several years after the hair cutting incident, she had the urge to travel. It was 1972, and Eunice was fourteen. Dunston, the upstate

New York town she lived in, wasn't tiny. It had a prominent university that acted as a magnet to the larger world, so that the town's population was made up of people from all over. Eunice, though, wasn't interested in the cosmopolitan flavor of the place she'd known all her life. She wanted out. And out she'd go. To Colorado.

A girl in her class used to live there and spoke of it lovingly, with a wistfulness that made Eunice ache. She wanted more than anything to love something completely and to leave herself behind.

She debated with herself about telling her parents she was going. She didn't debate long. Her mother cleaned houses for well-off people. She came home exhausted and surly. She hated her clients for their gracious homes, and the luxuries she deserved herself, even when they tipped her on holidays. Her father worked as a delivery man for a liquor store. His job also brought him in contact with the town's elite. He wasn't as cross as Eunice's mother, but he was jealous, too.

"Those folks drink first-rate hooch," he confided to Eunice more than once. "Just think of that!"

Eunice had never tasted alcohol and couldn't understand its wide appeal. Her parents drank, a lot, in fact, and then their words slurred and their voices rose and sometimes things hit the wall and broke.

Drinking was entering a state of voluntary madness, Eunice concluded. Sometimes, especially on weekends, that madness went on for a while. If she timed it right, her parents might not notice her absence until she was long gone.

The time was now!

The Wild West was calling.

Turned out that the West wasn't so wild after all. Denver had lots of shopping malls and freeways, bad traffic, and something Eunice had never seen— smog. Some days, the brown air made the Rockies look fake. Eunice rented a motel room by the week. The motel manager had asked how old she was, and she said she was eighteen. The manager clearly didn't believe her. He suspected she was there to turn tricks, but because she was alone, no shady male in the background to collect her wages, he let it go. Eunice was miserable in that motel room. She waited for the police to knock on her door, sent there by a long trail of phone calls and interviews with people who saw a young woman answering her description riding a cross country bus, but after five whole days, nothing happened. She walked all over, trying to get a sense of this new, sunny, dusty place. She ate in Mexican restaurants. She bought herself a cowboy hat. She was running through her money—carefully collected over the last year from her Grandma Grace, who was feeling her age and wanted to make amends for the daughter who became Eunice's mother. The gifts had come in bright, cheerful cards Grandma Grace knew Eunice's mother wouldn't think to open. Eunice thought she might get a job, assuming she could convince someone she was older than she was, but the newspaper offered little in the way of want ads. She hit a low point. Coming there was clearly a bad idea. She wasn't up to inventing herself out of whole cloth. She lay on her bed in the motel room and stared at the popcorn ceiling. She had just enough to buy a ticket home.

The thought of the long ride back didn't really bother her. Facing her parents did. She was mad that they hadn't found her, as if it was the most normal thing in the world for a girl her age to take herself off across country without a word. She intended to be cold and arrogant when she was once again under their roof. She'd make them feel as if she'd done them a favor by coming home. After all, what they needed most were her capable hands. The routine housework fell to her. She anticipated walking back into a mess of unwashed dishes and piled up laundry. Liquor bottles would line the kitchen counter. The trash would overflow. Thinking of her home in a state of increasing decay was upsetting. What if her parents had gone off the rails without her steadying influence?

What if they drank themselves into a stupor and lost their jobs? What then? Winter would come around again, as it always did. Heating oil wasn't cheap. They'd lived on state assistance more than once. Eunice supposed they could do so again, if they had to.

Eunice was surprised by her tears. She wasn't a crier. Kids who cried at school made her want to puke. Being a sissy never solved anything.

She put her clothes in her backpack, along with a few small things she'd bought for herself during her week in Denver. These included a string of lights shaped like chili peppers; an embroidered shirt from a thrift shop, with a nasty orange stain she'd tried and failed to wash out; and a pair of flimsy sunglasses that soon became scratched and cloudy.

A woman's voice, raised in strife, was audible next door. Eunice assumed she was yelling at someone else in the room—her husband, probably— but there was no answer to her punctuated wails. Who could stay silent against that kind of assault? She must be talking on the telephone, Eunice realized. Eunice opened the door to her own room and stepped out onto the balcony. She walked past the window, and sure enough, a woman was sitting on the bed with the phone to her ear. She was wearing a bathrobe. There were curlers in her hair. She held a lit cigarette between the fingers of her free hand.

"What do you expect me to do?" she screamed into the phone. She sat silently for a moment. Then she hung up without a word. Eunice stayed still, though now, with the phone conversation over and done, she felt like an intruder, where before she was merely observing.

The woman had thin, bony shoulders, visible through the fabric of her robe. The cords in her neck stood out. She didn't seem all that old, not as old as Eunice's mother, who was in her mid-forties. Eunice's mother often said that she had never planned to have children and that Eunice's arrival had been a complete surprise. Her tone suggested that the surprise had not been a welcome one.

A pick-up truck pulled into the parking lot below. Country music whined from its open windows. In her brief time there in the West, Eunice had developed a liking for country music. She could be a cowgirl, if she were both older and braver. The driver turned off the engine, and the music stopped. Eunice's neighbor turned her head in the direction of the sudden silence, saw Eunice, and stared at her with a dull, empty look. She stood and crossed the room. She opened the door.

"Don't stand out there like that. Come in, for Christ's sake!"

Eunice did as she was told.

The room had a fresh smell, maybe of cologne.

The woman took her seat on the bed. She had left the door open.

"Well?" the woman said, not looking at Eunice.

"Well, what?"

"Aren't you going to clean up?"

"I'm not the maid."

"Then who the hell are you?"

"I have the room next door."

The woman nodded, looking hollow and deflated once more. She crushed out her cigarette in the glass ashtray on the bed. Eunice's mother was a smoker, too. She set her bed clothes on fire once, because she'd been drinking and dropped a cinder on the spread. If she'd been asleep, they might all have burned up, but she was awake, *thinking*, she said.

"What's your name?" the woman asked.

Eunice hesitated.

"You have one, don't you?"

"Lillian."

"That's a lovely name."

"Thank you."

"My name's Doris. Which is an ugly name."

"Not really."

"Yes, really."

Doris pointed to the chair by the dresser and told Eunice to sit down. Eunice moved the clothes on the chair to the bottom of the bed. She sat.

"She says I can't see her anymore," Doris said.

"Who?"

"My daughter."

Doris wiped her nose with a piece of tissue she had in the pocket of her robe. She said the daughter had left home several months before. Doris—and the daughter—were from a little town called Roy.

"That's in Washington. State," Doris said. She wiped her nose again. She removed her curlers and continued talking.

The daughter, Lisa Sue, was of age, twenty-three to be exact. Lisa Sue didn't get along with Doris' husband, Lyall. Lyall wasn't Lisa Sue's father, just a guy who wanted to provide and protect. Things didn't go well. "Bad blood from day one," was how Doris put it. Lisa Sue had moved out of the house several years before and was living in Seattle, but she got sick of the rain and wanted to go somewhere dry. All of that was fine, hunky-dory in fact, except for one small problem: Lisa Sue refused to tell anyone where she was living, or even give out her phone number. She wanted to sever all contact with Doris and Lyall. "You're a sick couple of fucks," were her very words.

That made Doris think. Maybe something went on between Lyall and Lisa Sue that wasn't exactly above board. Lyall could be a little ... *expressive*, sometimes. Doris confronted Lyall. He told her she was full of crap. Then he moved out. Fourteen years of marriage down the drain on account of Lisa Sue who didn't want to be found. That kind of situation could be hard on a person, Doris said. She hired a detective to find Lisa Sue, which was pretty easy because she had different colored eyes and a birthmark on the back of one hand. And she liked dancing, and always talked of wanting to be a dancer—any kind of dancer—and since money wasn't all that easy to come by, she danced in a strip joint, which the detective referred to as a "gentlemen's club." Tracking her to Denver was easy, too, because a guy she used to go with moved back there when they broke up. Thinking about it now, Doris said she probably could have found her on her own but didn't have it in her to traipse through that sort of seedy establishment again and again.

Now Lisa Sue was threatening to call the law if Doris didn't leave her alone and get herself back up the pike to Roy.

"She's just got no idea what it's like, being a mother. And may God strike me dead, but the truth is, part of me hates her for the hurt she's caused," Doris said.

Eunice wondered if that's how her own mother had felt when she came home to find Eunice gone. About the hurt, not the wrath of God.

"She must figure I knew about Lyall and just didn't care. She couldn't be more wrong about that. I didn't know a damn thing. And if I did, I sure as hell wouldn't have stood by."

"What are you going to do?" Eunice asked.

"Go home. What else?"

Eunice didn't want to go home. She knew that now. She wanted to start over, just the way Lisa Sue had. Though at fourteen, how could she? It would take another four years to finish high school, and how would she live until then? She couldn't very well call up and ask her parents for money. The situation was impossible.

"Take me with you," Eunice said.

Doris stared at her, uncomprehending.

"I'm not any trouble, you'll see. I work hard. I just need a place to stay while I finish school. There's a school near where you live, isn't there? If not, I can take a bus, unless I can work out some other way to get around."

"Where are your parents?"

"I ran away."

"And you've been staying here, at the motel?"

241

"Yes. Now I'm out of money. I was going back today—just about to head out to the bus station when I heard you on the phone."

Eunice could see Doris' thoughts turn inward again.

To fill up the growing silence from Doris, Eunice told her everything, even about cutting her hair all those years before.

"And you haven't called them? They don't know where you are?" Doris asked.

"No."

"That's pretty harsh. Even a lousy parent worries when their kid takes off."

Eunice said nothing. She refused to feel guilty.

"Besides, I don't even know you," Doris said.

"I'm just like anybody else."

"That covers a lot of ground."

Again, Doris paused.

"What's your favorite food?" she asked.

"Fried chicken and mashed potatoes."

"Sounds reasonable. Have you ever been in trouble with the law?"

"No."

"Do you go out with boys?"

"No."

"Don't you have any friends you'll miss a lot back home?"

"Not really."

"You need to call your parents, at least tell them that you're okay. And be prepared for the fact that they might exert their rights and call the police to bring you back. You won't be able to do anything about it."

"Only if they figure out where I am, and I don't intend on telling them."

Some spark of recognition registered in Doris' eyes, as if she admired Eunice's cunning and clear thinking.

"Aren't you worried about getting in a car with some woman you don't know anything about?" Doris asked. She was on her feet then, putting her clothes in a banged-up looking suitcase.

"I know enough to know that you're probably not a nut."

"Well, I better not find out that *you're* a nut."

"I'm not."

"And if it doesn't work out—if we don't get along under the same roof—I'll give you the money to go back home, and I'll make sure you get there."

Eunice figured that Doris was talking tough at that point to make herself feel better about Lisa Sue.

243

"I keep a tidy place; you should know that right off. I can't stand dirt, and I can't stand mess," Doris said.

"Fine with me."

Doris looked at Eunice in a cold, thoroughly appraising way. She seemed on the verge of changing her mind.

"One thing you should know. My name's not really Lillian," Eunice said.

"What is it?"

"Eunice."

"That was my mother's name."

"See? It's karma."

"I don't believe in karma. But I do believe in second chances, which is more than I can say for some people."

Eunice could see Doris thinking about Lisa Sue again.

"Go back to your room, call home, and be nice about it," Doris said.

Eunice looked at the clock and pushed the time two hours ahead in her mind. Her parents were supposed to be at work. But if one of them should answer, she'd hang up the phone. She couldn't bear to hear a familiar voice right then. For some strange reason, having her future open up, now that Doris had agreed to take her along, made her feel lonely as hell, worse than at any point since she left home. But she dialed the operator and asked to place a collect call, and let the phone ring five times until the operator asked if she'd like to try her call again later.

Eunice sat down on the bed. The strength seemed to have gone out of her. She lifted the receiver of the telephone again and asked the operator to dial a different number. Grandma Grace answered, said she'd accept the charges, and then said, "Child, I thought you were dead."

Eunice was sure Grandma Grace was seated in one of her kitchen table chairs with the yellow vinyl seats and metal legs. The entire room appeared before her with its faded daisy-patterned wallpaper, the windowsill over the sink crowded with flowering plants, the ancient electric clock above the stove that hummed to itself all day long and into the dead of night. She'd be in a dress and apron, and a pair of worn slippers. The one bracelet she wore, with charms collected long ago, would have slid down her arm as she held the phone to her ear.

"I'm sorry," Eunice said.

"I don't blame you one bit for going. But I wished you'd let me know beforehand. I'm an old woman with an old woman's tired heart. You about did me in."

Again, Eunice said she was sorry. She explained the situation with Doris, making it sound like they'd met when Eunice first came to the motel.

"What will you do for money?" Grandma Grace asked.

Eunice said she didn't know.

"You don't plan to ask that woman for it, do you?"

Eunice agreed that that would be a bad idea.

"Tell you what. You send me an address, and I'll make sure you get a little allowance. God knows where I'll get it from, but I'll manage."

She always talked like that, though she wasn't badly off. It was common knowledge that her late husband fenced stolen stereos and guns, even a car now and then, out of the back of his auto repair shop. He made a decent, if illegal, living. Then he died in the middle of a card game, playing for the keys to a hot motorcycle.

Eunice saw herself waiting for the mail at Doris' house, opening Grandma Grace's letters , putting money in her dresser drawer. Someday there'd be a whole lot in there, because she was a frugal person and used to doing without. She'd write letters in return about the new life she'd found on the other side of the world from Dunston. She would never look back, never think about the town she left behind, or the pair that made her leave.

The plan was made, they said their good-byes and hung up. It didn't occur to Eunice until she and Doris were well into Wyoming that neither she nor Grandma Grace had once mentioned Eunice's parents.

*

The Roy episode, as she came to think of it, somewhat followed the plot of Lillian Gish's debut film, *An Unseen Enemy*, where an unscrupulous housekeeper tries to steal an inheritance locked in a safe. Only it wasn't money that was at stake, but Eunice herself. The safe she was locked within was one of ignorance, and fortified by wanting so much to belong.

That wasn't easy. Newcomers in Roy were rare, regarded with suspicion. Arriving in the summer meant that Eunice had nothing to do until school started. Doris worked as a caregiver in a nursing home. At the end of the day, she was tired yet cheerful. She cooked dinner, then washed up. She didn't ask Eunice to help and didn't let her, even when she offered to. Eunice was given a small bedroom off the kitchen, a former shed that had been attached to the main house the year before and supplied with a free-standing electric heater. Lisa Sue had planned to use it as some sort of art studio, though which art she practiced wasn't clear until Eunice, in a fit of boredom, went through a box at the back of the hall closet and found some inept charcoal drawings, all of a man—the same man— wearing horns. Eunice assumed that the subject was Lyall, Doris' estranged husband.

Doris sensed Eunice's restlessness. Eunice was a young girl with a young girl's energy, and Doris had made a mistake by assuming that staying on her own day after day out in the country would make her happy. She sat at her small kitchen table, shoulders hunched, just as she had in the Denver motel room, and recited a list of other mistakes she'd made in her thirty-eight years. First was probably being born, though that wasn't something she had any control over. Next was being only of average intelligence, for had she had more gray matter, as she put it, she would have gone farther in this life. Then came getting pregnant at the age of fifteen, a misery she hoped to hell Eunice would have the good sense to avoid. Keeping the baby had gone against the advice of just about everyone, including her own mother, who'd had the good grace to die by the time Doris was only twenty-two.

"Lung cancer," Doris said, solemnly, as she ground out the cigarette she'd smoked down to the filter line.

Along came Lyall, like a knight in shining armor, who convinced her that what she needed was a man to give her a home. The home in question being that dump they were sitting in right then. Eunice was surprised to hear Doris speak badly of her house. The way she took care of it, dusting and vacuuming every day, you'd think she looked upon it as a damn palace. Lyall wasn't bad, and things were pretty spiffy in the beginning, though just when Doris thought they made a pretty nice little family, Lisa Sue, entering the darkness of her teenage years, started acting up. And well, Eunice knew the rest.

She did indeed. On the drive north from Colorado, Doris had treated her to a monologue about her many disappointments. Eunice assumed that this was what lonely people did once they found a bit of company. Mile after mile, she heard Grandma Grace's voice in her ear, as if she were there in the station wagon, listening, too.

Oh, dry up, you damn crybaby!

Doris ran out of steam and sat for a while staring through the screen door into the yard. She sat until the light turned blue, an evening shade Eunice hadn't witnessed before, and was due, she thought, to the northern latitude. During her many long afternoons alone, she had pored over the few books Doris possessed, one of which was a world Atlas from 1946.

Then Doris stood and left the kitchen. In the morning, she told Eunice to get dressed and come into work with her. She'd tell her boss that Eunice was actually sixteen and was therefore legally able to work twenty hours a week.

Eunice had no interest in taking care of old people. As far as she was concerned, she'd overseen her parents' nonsense so much that she never wanted to be in charge of anyone ever again. She was given no choice.

Pine Ridge was a Medicaid facility. There was a much nicer nursing home down in Tacoma that was private, expensive, and picky about whom they hired. It was the kind of place Doris dreamed of being able to live in one day, herself. There was nothing about Doris that suggested the old woman she might become, and Eunice found it really weird that she'd even think in those terms. It was like Eunice planning for middle-age. Right then all she could entertain was her fifteenth birthday that would take place that fall. Would her parents remember the day? Would they grieve anew at her disappearance? Had they grieved at all? What Eunice had come to realize was that it was she who grieved her own departure. She actually missed Dunston. She even missed her parents on occasion. Those moments had increased with annoying frequency. She told herself she was being a stupid sap. She tried to remember all the bad times instead. Sometimes Doris asked about those bad times, sensing that they were without number, but Eunice said nothing. Doris was the talker, not she. Doris, like movie audiences of old, would have to content herself with silence.

The men and women in Doris' care were small, white, and shriveled, like cauliflowers with skin. Eunice wore the same beige pants and flowered smock that Doris had, only the flowers on hers were blue while Doris' were red. The color was used to designate responsibility, Doris explained. Red flowers meant you knew how to get someone in and out of bed without letting them fall; blue flowers meant you could empty the trash, adjust the blinds, and dust the furniture. Eunice didn't believe that these divisions were set in stone, but she didn't argue because she had no interest in having any sort of physical contact with the residents. Yet sometimes it couldn't be avoided. One woman put her gnarled hand on Eunice's arm when Eunice was straightening a pile of magazines on the nightstand that clearly hadn't been moved for some time. The skin on that hand was smooth. The touch was light. One man patted her on the head as she stooped in front of his wheelchair to pick up the reading glasses he'd dropped. Again, a light touch. Eunice felt so strange, there on her knees, as if the man were blessing her. She certainly didn't feel blessed. Blessed was not a word she used.

The only time Doris let Eunice out of her sight was at lunch, when Eunice stole herself into the back garden to eat her bologna sandwich in peace. She didn't mind the nursing home, really, and picking up a few dollars was no drawback either. It was Doris watching her all the time that she came to hate. Doris knew that, too, and sulked. She apologized for being such a mother hen, then begged Eunice to understand her situation. She was still heart-broken over Lisa Sue, sometimes to the point of madness. She used that exact word. She was different then from the woman in the Denver motel room who, though racked with tears, had shown a solid practical streak that was much less in evidence there in Roy.

At the start of the second week, Doris let Eunice work by herself. She had a wobbly cleaning cart she wheeled up and down the silent halls. She replaced toilet paper in the bathroom and wiped down the plastic shower stall with a liquid cleanser that burned her hands until she thought to wear a pair of rubber gloves she found in the storeroom. The gloves were too big and easily filled with water that left her skin as wrinkled as the men and women who sat by, still as statues. No one talked to her. The other care workers were too busy, and the younger ones, closer to her own age, were cynical and hard, as if working among the soon-to-be-dead was firm proof that all of one's efforts only came to nothing in the end.

One girl, Janine, made time to chat with her, though. She thought Eunice was Doris' niece. Eunice said that was correct, figuring Doris had made up the story to keep people from asking questions that might eventually lead to finding out that she was a runaway.

Janine was even skinnier than Eunice, and a lot taller. She had a long, mournful face, though she was cheerful most of the time. The home was a summer job until she went away to college in the fall. She didn't seem to think it was so bad working around old people, except when they got all whiny and sad about the families that never visited.

"You do for folks all your life, and they blow you off when you're too old to have any teeth left and all your marbles are gone, too; I say fuck 'em," Janine said. She was enjoying her egg salad sandwich. Mayonnaise stuck to the edge of her lip. Eunice tapped her own lip to indicate this. Janine daintily dabbed her mouth on a napkin.

"Better not to have any," Janine said.

"Any what?"

"Kids, of course. Fucking ingrates they all turn out to be, at least if you listen to these poor souls."

Eunice had trouble thinking of the home's residents as poor souls. They had everything done for them. If they didn't want to hobble off to the dining room, a tray was brought to their room. Their clothes got washed, volunteers showed up and read to them, they even had a movie night, for God's sake! Didn't seem like a bad life to Eunice. Sometimes she wondered if Grandma Grace would end up in a home, too. Grandma Grace had too much pride for that, Eunice was sure. She would never let anyone handle her or spoon food into her mouth.

Janine talked about going to college somewhere in eastern Washington. She was both looking forward to it and apprehensive at the same time.

"I'm not too good with change," she said. She crumpled up her lunch sack and tossed it into the open metal container by the door. She clapped when it went in. It was a good distance away.

Eunice thought about the changes she'd endured in just a few weeks. She was in a sticky sort of limbo, she decided. Maybe when fall came and she started school she would feel more at home. Roy was so strange, ringed with enormous evergreen trees, yet the lawns were all brown. She had asked Doris about this—why the grass wasn't green—and Doris shrugged. The same worn world atlas that told her how far north she was also had a map depicting rainfall and general humidity levels. The West was dry, even that close to the ocean.

The grass in Dunston stayed green all summer. Then it was buried by snow. It didn't snow much in Roy, apparently. Up in the mountains, sure. But Roy was practically at sea level.

"It's a strange place, isn't it?" Eunice asked.

"What is?"

"Roy."

"Not really. I'm used to it. Aren't you used to it? Doris said you basically grew up here, then moved away to Spokane for a while, and came back when your folks died."

"She told you all that."

"Sad story."

"Sure is."

"Anyhow, maybe you're just seeing it with fresh eyes and all."

"Maybe."

The afternoon went on; Eunice cleaned rooms and avoided looking at Doris whenever they passed in the halls. Doris bought a frozen pizza at the store on the way home because she didn't feel like cooking. She was in one of those sad, silent moods that seemed to come out of nowhere. Eunice didn't mind. They ate without a word, and when Doris went to watch television, as she always did, Eunice sat in her room and thought.

She wanted to call Grandma Grace but knew that Doris would hear her and eavesdrop. Then she'd interrogate her about the conversation in a way that would make it seem like Eunice was committing an act of betrayal.

"This is nuts," Eunice said to the wood-paneled walls around her.

The next morning, Eunice stayed in bed. Doris put her hand on her forehead and announced that she felt warm. Eunice had applied the electric heat pad to her face a number of times that morning, and now the heat pad was buried beneath the blanket, which she wanted more than anything to kick off. The heat pad was kept in the upstairs hall. Eunice had had to move slowly in the night to get it without causing the old boards to creak, because Doris always bragged about being a light sleeper, but by the time Eunice was halfway up the steps, her snores sounded like furniture being scraped across a bare floor, which gave her the confidence to trot lightly the rest of the way.

"I'll stay home, too, and make you some nice chicken soup," Doris said.

"No! We can't both let them down. It wouldn't

be fair." Eunice spoke softly and with effort, as if in pain.

She could see Doris consider. Doris didn't love her job, but she didn't want to lose it, especially after the time she took off to go to Denver, though she could probably afford to. Eunice had learned that Lyall, for all of his alleged faults, paid the mortgage on the place even though he no longer lived there.

"All right. But I'll call you and check in," Doris said.

"Oh, please don't do that. I don't want to have to get out of bed to answer the phone."

Again, Doris considered. It was true that the phone was in the kitchen, a bit of a walk from Eunice's makeshift room. It was the only one in the house. Most people liked to have a phone in their bedrooms, but not Doris. Maybe she was afraid that it would ring late at night, heralding some awful news.

"I'll leave early then," Doris said.

Eunice nodded weakly and gave her best brave smile. She deepened her gaze to underscore the depth of her suffering and courage, but Doris had turned away by then.

Doris' station wagon rumbled down the driveway. Soon there was only silence. Eunice got out of bed, went into the kitchen, and put water on her face. She actually felt ill, both from the artificial heat she'd had to use to persuade Doris and because the idea of going back to Dunston sat badly. But she had no choice. It was now or never. Just the week before, when Eunice had made the mistake of wondering what the summer was like that year in Dunston, Doris said she had to forget all about that place, that there was absolutely no returning now, and that if Eunice should get a notion and run off, Doris would call the law and say she was a danger to herself. She said it with a little smile, but there was steel behind the words. Doris meant to keep her. Eunice knew Doris was powerless, but she didn't want a scene. She couldn't stand tears and recriminations. Doris had enough grief, even though Eunice had come to realize that she'd caused a lot of it herself.

Lillian would have been kind in this way, too: seeing a person's fault and then protecting it. Eunice didn't know anything about Lillian Gish, though, did she? A small woman with a small pretty face—the same as Eunice, though she couldn't vouch for the prettiness of her face, only that she was small, too. She'd put on no height since coming to Roy. She'd stood up against a door frame and marked where her head met the wood with a pencil, then she took a yardstick she found in a closet and determined that she was still five feet three inches tall. Doris was a lot taller, maybe three or four inches, but she was wiry. She had to be, to wrestle some of those old people in and out of bed.

Getting to the bus depot would require the use of the old bicycle behind the garage. Eunice had checked to make sure the tires weren't flat. She'd have to leave the bicycle there, which she regretted but couldn't help. Her backpack would be no fuller than it had been when she arrived, since she hadn't bought herself any clothes. There was no place to shop in Roy, in any case, except the grocery store and the gas station. She had eighty dollars that Grandma Grace had sent in two separate cards that Eunice snatched from the mailbox before Doris could get there. The mailbox was at the end of their long dirt road, and Eunice, during the many days there on her own, learned what time of day the carrier tended to drive by. The arrangement had been that one card would be sent each month on the fourth—something to do with the arrival of Grandma Grace's Social Security checks. The last card had arrived the week before, which meant that another one wouldn't go out until after Eunice had arrived back in Dunston. Eunice thought it best to call Grandma Grace collect from the bus depot anyway and bring her up to date on her change of plans. Grandma Grace didn't answer the phone. Eunice very much wished that she had.

The bus wasn't very full until Spokane; then a lot of people boarded heading for some convention in Chicago. A number of them were drunk. The smell of alcohol reminded Eunice of what she was returning to. She thought of Doris finding her note that said only *Sorry it didn't work out*. She made no mention of the bicycle because she assumed Doris had forgotten all about it. She ate the cheese sandwich she had made at the house. The bus stopped in some small town in western Montana so everyone could freshen up. The night was coming on slowly, and back on board, Eunice fell asleep.

Doris read her note and sat weeping quietly, just as she had when Eunice first saw her. It wasn't Doris, though, but the woman in the seat next to Eunice, suffering some unspoken grief of her own that seemed so dire that Eunice pretended she had never awakened and was still fast asleep.

Eunice tried Grandma Grace again when the bus stopped in Wisconsin. Still no answer. Eunice was on edge. It wasn't like Grandma Grace not to pick up. Had she taken herself on a little vacation? She often spoke of Florida, and walking barefoot in the warm, wet sand. The idea of Grandma Grace tiptoeing on the beach made Eunice smile and helped keep her thoughts positive the rest of the way.

When Eunice had left Dunston, the season had

just begun to rise; now summer had settled heavily. The thick, green leaves cast a sleepy shade on the flat streets of downtown. Eunice went right to Grandma Grace's house. The unwatered plants in the window boxes brought a renewed sense of alarm. Her frantic knock was unanswered. She peered through the window of the back door. The kitchen was in order, except that two of the four chairs at the table were pulled out as if someone was about to sit—or had risen in a hurry.

Eunice sat for a moment on the back stairs to collect herself. The long ride coupled with the disappointment of not finding Grandma Grace made her fists clench and unclench until she told herself to calm down, go home, and then get to the bottom of things. The walk across town might steady her nerves.

On a main street, a girl in a passing car leaned from the rolled down window and called Eunice's name. Eunice waved, trying to remember which of her classes the girl had been in. No one was particularly nice to her at school, and Eunice generally kept to herself, though sometimes people said "Hi" when they passed her in the halls. Grandma Grace said Eunice had a kind face, which was worth a lot in this world, almost as much as one's spirit or soul, not that she was a religious person in any way. To Grandma Grace, spirit and soul informed one's

261

character, which in turn determined how one met and conquered adversity. Eunice's mother had no character, Grandma Grace stated more than once. Eunice's father wasn't much better, but he had a good heart. "Weakness is chosen, not inherited," she liked to say.

Eunice was shocked to feel such pleasure at the sight of her own house. It still needed paint and new front stairs, and the yard was as overgrown as ever, but it really didn't look so bad. She was glad to arrive in the daytime. She wasn't up to confronting her parents just yet.

But there they were, sitting at the kitchen table. Her mother's hair was hidden by a scarf, which meant her hair hadn't been washed in several days. They stared at her.

"Well, look who it is," Eunice's mother said. Eunice realized with a jolt of terror that her mother was sober—they both were.

"What are you guys doing here?" Eunice asked.

"Could ask you the same thing. Didn't figure you'd be back," Eunice's mother said.

"Stop that, Louise. Give us a hug, girl," Eunice's father said.

Eunice didn't budge. The straps of her backpack pulled painfully on her shoulders, something she hadn't noticed while she'd been in motion.

"Where's Grandma Grace?" Eunice asked.

"Haven't you heard?" Eunice's mother asked.

"How could I have heard anything?"

"Right. She said she knew where you were, but since she never told us, there was no way to get the news to you."

"What the hell happened?"

"Hospital. Fell and broke her hip. We each got a couple of days off. Family emergency and all."

"Can I go see her?"

"Just as soon as you do some fancy explaining about how come you took off without a word."

Eunice sat. She didn't remove her backpack.

Eunice's mother stared at her coldly. Then she stood up, pushed in her chair, and left the kitchen.

"Don't let her rattle you," Eunice's father said. He patted the back of Eunice's hand.

"She hates me. She always has. I don't know why the hell I even came back."

"She doesn't hate you. You gave her a bad turn is all."

"Weren't you worried about me, too?"

"Sure I was! But I knew you'd be okay. Also knew you'd come back when you realized that whatever you were looking for wasn't so easy to find."

263

He looked her in the eye for a long moment that made Eunice uneasy.

"You're all right, then," he said. Eunice nodded.

He gazed into an empty cup that may have held coffee. Eunice studied his face. She wanted to see if it had changed. She saw nothing new. He looked exhausted.

He told her not to worry. He understood. He'd had a hard mother, too, someone who made him feel as if he could never really measure up. Always comparing him to his older brother who got killed in a car wreck the night he graduated from high school. Even after his brother died, and Eunice's father was all she had left, his mother put him down. One day, he took off, only to return like Eunice, wishing things had changed in his absence. But, nothing had. Eunice was lucky, he said. For her, things were on a definite upswing.

"Why?" she asked.

"Your mom quit drinking."

"Again."

"It's something."

"Why did she?"

Eunice's father ran his hand over the back of his head. Eunice had seen him do this many times, usually when her mother had asked him why he was such an idiot or why he couldn't provide better for his family.

"Felt like it was time for a change, I guess," he said.

Eunice knew this change, like all the others, would be short-lived. She wanted to believe, even so, that she was the cause of her mother's temporary improvement, that her being away had made her sit down and think. Whatever the reason, her mother would have bullied her father into giving up the booze, too, so she wouldn't have to go it alone. For the moment, with two clear-headed parents at the helm, Eunice felt overwhelmed. The household would be reorganized along whatever manic lines her mother devised, until the effort became too much, and she'd hit the bottle again.

"What say you freshen up, and we'll all go out and pay your grandma a nice visit?" Eunice's father asked.

"Sure."

Eunice climbed the narrow stairs to her room, which was exactly as she'd left it months before, down to the unmade bed and moldy bath towel she'd dropped on the floor, which had managed to dry to crust in the time ensuing. The only thing new was a thicker layer of dust over her dresser and nightstand. With her forefinger, she traced L.

*

During the next four years, as Eunice stumbled unwilling through high school, it was Grandma Grace who perfected the look of longing and pain. The broken hip laid her up for a good six months, during which a string of sullen and inept homecare workers came and went through her kitchen door. On her feet again, Grandma Grace was a changed woman. Gone was the brassy tone and sharp tongue Eunice had known all her life. What replaced it were long stretches of silence accompanied by a furious gaze that bore through whatever it fell upon—even Eunice, who felt clumsy and inadequate. Once, she asked Grandma Grace what she'd done wrong.

"Who says you did anything wrong?"

"The way you look at me."

"I'm not aware of looking at you in any particular way."

Eunice knew Grandma Grace had meant no harm.

When the supply of care workers dried up, Eunice took over Grandma Grace's care. Though she got around reasonably well, Grandma Grace was clearly terrified of another fall. So Eunice cleaned her house, changed the sheets on her bed, did the laundry, and even bought groceries when her father had time to drive her to the store, which had to be scheduled during the narrow window between the end of his work day and the start of his evening revelry. He now roosted in their living room, watching the same television where Eunice had discovered Lillian Gish all those years before. Her mother had claimed the kitchen table for her daily binge. Eunice passed by them, receiving scant acknowledgment, sometimes a request for another bottle of beer or a clean ashtray or to take out the trash.

"What are you going to do with your life?" Grandma Grace asked Eunice one afternoon.

"I don't know."

"Nonsense. You're almost eighteen years old. You have to have some idea."

Eunice shrugged. She unpacked the two grocery bags she'd brought in. She now had a driver's license and used Grandma Grace's old Buick to go back and forth.

"How can I, when I'm not good at anything?" Eunice asked.

"You're good at taking care of people."

Eunice supposed that that was true. She'd taken care of her parents for years, she'd worked a little while at the nursing home in Roy, and she'd been at Grandma Grace's side almost constantly, so much so that they'd talked about her moving in and leaving her parents behind.

"But it might not be the best work for a young woman. Not right off, anyhow. Go out and see the world first."

"I did that, remember? Far as I can tell, the world is pretty much the same anywhere as it is here."

"Maybe." Grandma Grace paused to shuffle the worn deck of cards she always had in the pocket of her sweater. She could play solitaire for hours.

"Besides, who would take care of you?" Eunice asked. She put a can of tuna fish on the counter as a reminder to herself to use it later to make sandwiches for lunch.

"I'll find someone."

They had this conversation about once a month, and it always ended with them dropping it until the next time.

"What about boys?" Grandma Grace asked. This was a new tack, and it caught Eunice off guard.

"What about them?"

"Don't you like any?"

"No."

Eunice had had a terrible crush on Brad Chalmers in her math class the year before. He was spectacularly handsome, and incredibly stupid.

Whenever he spoke, people laughed, and the poor thing turned red. Eunice felt his pain. She knew what it was like to be laughed at. She decided that they were peas in a pod, two survivors stranded on the cruel island of Dunston High School, alone against the world.

"We can face it together, you know," Eunice once summoned the courage to tell him when she cornered him by his locker.

"Face what?" he asked. Up close she noticed a number of flaws, like one nostril being smaller than the other and a tiny pimple under one eye, but it was the fact that his breath stank that put her off. Her crush faded then and there. She'd chided herself for a while afterwards, thinking herself shallow, unworthy of real love because she'd been so easily deterred by a problem easily fixed with mouthwash or a roll of mints.

In the end, she thought it was destiny, and she accepted her solitary state with the same courage she'd found to leave and then return home.

But her reckless, hungry heart would not be kept still, and another boy soon caught her eye: Larry Lester, a bad sort, Grandma Grace would say, only wanting a girl for one thing. Which Eunice gave him willingly under the bleachers after school one day. When her period was late, she panicked, looked up the laws about getting an abortion, and cried with relief when her period showed up in the middle of the following week. The use of birth control didn't occur to her until later, when Larry had moved on to another girl, and yet another one after that.

"Well, men have their uses, you know," Grandma Grace said. "Just you keep an open mind."

Grandma Grace told a tale she'd told many times before, about being courted by her late husband. He came to her house with flowers, then sang beneath her window with a guitar he played so badly that her father chased him off with a shotgun. Only then did Grandma Grace's expression lighten, before quickly becoming dark and brooding once again.

Not long after, Grandma Grace died in her sleep. It wasn't Eunice who found her, but a neighbor Grandma Grace had invited over for coffee in a rare mood of hospitality. Eunice took it as a sign—not the death, which was inevitable, but Grandma Grace's change of heart about having people in her home. That Grandma Grace had left her house and bank accounts to Eunice, rather than to Eunice's mother, proved that life contained a number of unexpected possibilities that one should be ready to embrace. Of the roughly three hundred thousand dollars that Eunice received, including proceeds from the sale of the house, she gave ten thousand to her father alone, in recognition of the fact that he did truly care for her, though seldom showed it. To her mother, she gave nothing, despite being treated to a daily rant about her disgusting ingratitude and monstrous selfishness.

She sought then, as she had four years before, to get away and leave Dunston behind. She'd go first to Florida, where she'd walk on the beach with the spirit of Grandma Grace at her side. She'd guard her fortune with great care. She'd find any decent job available, live modestly, and reach out to others with an open heart. No more turning her back on life, she thought. Something good would come her way.

about the author

Anne Leigh Parrish is the author of *What Nell Dreams*, a novella & stories (Unsolicited Press 2020); *Maggie's Ruse*, a novel(Unsolicited Press 2019); *The Amendment*, a novel (Unsolicited Press, 2017); *Women Within*, a novel (Black Rose Writing, 2017); *What Is Found, What Is Lost*, a novel (She Writes Press, 2014); *Our Love Could Light The World*, stories (She Writes Press, 2013); and *All The Roads That Lead From Home*, stories (Press 53, 2011). Her short stories have been published widely in literary venues. Her essays have appeared in *Book Riot, BookTrib, Writer's Digest,* and *Women Writers, Womens Books*.

about the press

Unsolicited Press was founded in 2012 and is based in Portland, Oregon. The small press publishes fiction, poetry, and creative nonfiction written by award-winning authors.

Learn more at www.unsolicitedpress.com

www.ingramcontent.com/pod-product-compliance
Lightning Source LLC
Chambersburg PA
CBHW030653260626
47157CB00007B/2625